LEONARD COHEN

LEONARD
COHEN

A Novel

JEFFREY LEWIS

First published in 2024 by
HAUS PUBLISHING LTD.
4 Cinnamon Row, London SW11 3TW

ISBN 978-1-913368-92-0
eISBN 978-1-913368-93-7

Distributed in North America by The University of Chicago Press

Typeset in Garamond by MacGuru Ltd
Printed in the United Kingdom by TJ Books Ltd, Padstow, Cornwall

A CIP catalogue for this book is available from the British Library

www.hauspublishing.com

et visent longas Capitolia pompas
Ovid

Dear Leonard Cohen,

Could I ask you something, just between us? How was it that you never changed your name? You could have been Lawrence Cole. You could have been Lindsay Kohl, or Lionel Cone. Or you could have dropped your last name and been Lenny Norman. Jewish entertainers do that one all the time, drop their last name, go by their middle name. But you, no, you couldn't do that. Sound less Jewish? Sound more like a show-biz guy? Not you, you had to be authentic, you had to sound like an accountant or a dentist. I'm joking, really, kind of. But not completely, not entirely. And now it's a little on the late side to do anything about it, isn't it? You see, I, too, am Leonard Cohen. And this has been a problem.

Not for the first twenty-two years of my life, it wasn't. I'd never heard of you. I grew up in peaceful middle-class American bliss, or narcosis if you must, Ashkenazic division, in upstate New York, in Rochester, where it snows so much it's almost like your Montreal. We were almost neighbors, if you think about it that way, which I often have. Neighbors across the great lake or up the great river. Lenny and Lenny, unknown to each other. Were you a Lenny? I was. Never a Len.

As for a middle name, I was Leonard Stuart Cohen. Leonard S. Cohen. Not that anybody knew anybody's middle name. But it's a sort of distinction, isn't it? Leonard Norman Cohen versus Leonard Stuart Cohen, Leonard N. Cohen versus Leonard S.

Cohen. If I'd known then what I know now, that sort of thing.

For twenty-two years my life was my own. I failed with girls, I watched my parents' marriage dissolve, I played my guitar. It was on Hydra, my first trip to Greece, first trip anywhere really, the summer of my graduation, when I first heard of you. More on that later, but enough to say for now you were just getting started then, you'd left the island and Marianne to be back in New York to begin your assault on the heights of the musical universe. Sorry, I can't think of a better phrase, "musical universe," but anyway that's what it was, wasn't it? 1968. Big doings in the world. Everything on the brink, or that's what some people thought anyway.

But for me, that summer, it all started with finding out that there was another Leonard Cohen, who played the guitar, who wrote songs, who was out there, on his way.

I've always hated to be embarrassed. And it was embarrassing to be "the other." Someone whose life was preempted, whose life became a shadow, meet anybody, "Oh, you're Leonard Cohen? Ha-ha," a life lived in reference to another. I suppose it could be true, too, of all the Elizabeth Taylors around, there's got to be a lot of Elizabeth Taylors, but even there the difference would be, in my opinion, that Leonard Cohen is so specific. Elizabeth Taylors, you'd expect there would be Elizabeth Taylors, it's almost a generic name, look up the Taylors in the phone book, there's got to be a ton more of them than Cohens, even in New York. I even looked a little like you when I was young. Dark, eyebrows, hungry. Conceivably a little mournful, from which I could break out a big smile every now and then just to keep it all off-balance. This brings me, a little anyway, to the other reason I would be writing you. I followed you sufficiently through your illustrious career to believe that you're someone who is an aficionado of miracles. Or at least you're willing to give them a chance, their day in court, so to speak. What temperament would be better suited

2

than yours, the cynical and the credulous all mixed up, a willing-
ness to suspend disbelief all the way down? Suspending disbelief,
I understand people say that about books, but for people like you
and me, isn't it more about a faith that takes us by surprise? My
story is what some would call a miracle. I would call it, simply,
love. Me, Lenny, big shot, love.

Yours,

Leonard

2

In the early days of August the *meltemi* blew strong and the sea bucked the old ferry and tossed it around and on the deck of the *Hellenic Maiden* hippies and gypsies and the middle-aged giving it a last fling held on in the dark and spray and wiped the salt from their eyes and enough of them sang as if the ship were going down. There had been a ship go down, the Crete car ferry a couple of years before, its great doors in neglect left unlocked and flung open and that was that, but the *Hellenic Maiden* was doing no more than giving its customers a ride. Inside, in the "classes," natives who had never absorbed the sea vomited in their chairs and the toilets overflowed, but on the soaking, sloshing deck it was a time of people's lives. Affairs were plotted, arguments for humanity's future were made, community was found or lost, and Leonard played his guitar.

He was hardly alone. There were others with guitars and there were harmonicas and someone with a zither sat on a stack of life rings and played Harry Lime's theme and each of these had their followers arrayed around them so that the only order to any of it was as a cacophonous prayer, its dissonance all in all. The *Maiden* was running late. A few who were destined for the more distant islands unrolled their sleeping rolls and angled for sleep and the gypsies tripped over them or pricked their air mattresses with pins. Leonard played whatever those around him sang, doleful and drunk on *retsina* and *raki* and the spray, as one after another the dark humps of the islands took form out of the Aegean night, sleeping animals of the sea. Then trucks would chug onto light-strewn quays, backpackers would troop off and on like prisoners in an exchange, and finally the ferry doors would clang shut and it was off once more on the rollercoaster waves, a voyage arguably more about what they were leaving behind than what they were approaching. Leonard slipped down a Dramamine. Others pawed the air and an American couple spontaneously remembered old Kingston Trio lyrics, as if more innocent times implausibly loomed. It was past midnight when he counted down the ferry's calls and knew that S. was next. There wasn't a harbor dredged for the ferries on S. so a *caique* came out to get them and people tumbled into the *caique* with their backpacks first and last so that what was created was a heap of humanity in the bottom of a leaky boat plus Leonard's guitar which he held with an arm stretched stiff over his head as if the guitar would be the last to drown. They reached the port at three and he found a beach just past where the *caique* beached and slept what was left of the night.

In the morning he washed his face in the sea and picked up the bits of canvas and clothing he had slept on and wandered into the town and the first café he found with a working toilet he put his pack and his guitar down. It was on S. that he was to meet his friends in five days' time because the friends had heard there were Danish girls to be found here, but there were no Danish girls around and it was eight o'clock and the sun was beating down. Leonard considered especially the chance his friends had been mistaken in choosing S. He drank his coffee sweet and rubbed his eyes and was oracular with himself when there was no one to contradict him. Then he wandered off. It was a Cycladic town that hugged its port in an old embrace, a town of refuge anciently Christian and white, as if guaranteeing itself with a show of modesty. No gaudy umbrellas defaced the modest esplanade nor gun emplacements the *kástro* and Leonard climbed the whitewashed steps and ducked through the urinous alleys and then he descended onto a single row of shops, a butcher, a dry goods shop, a place for bicycle tires and hardware, a grocery, a kiosk, a storefront where it was hard to tell what was on offer as there was nothing in the window but a cat, and at the narrow corner where the commercial strip angled back to the esplanade, at the terminus of this row of enterprise, a building that looked squeezed and punished, so stuffed on its narrow lot that having a door to enter allowed scarcely width for a selling window at all, which, straightened as it was, displayed little more than maps of the island, blank airmail notebooks, and a spray of Pelican Shakespeares. On the door hung a handprinted sign on a string, 'English Bookstore', and he went in.

It was a shop that felt as if it had shriveled and dried in the sun and it was comfortingly dark and hard to move in the aisles, so he left his pack and his guitar by the desk. The girl at the desk nodded and kept to herself, adding figures on an ancient adding machine. Leonard felt enwombed, as if he had found a familiar place. He made his way through the Pelicans and Penguins and guidebooks to the stacks of Durrell and Henry Miller, in that year 1968 the explainers of place and spirit to the arrivals from the north with their power and melancholy and money, then after these there was a box of records and he stopped to browse. He was the shop's only customer, he could have been the first of the day, it wasn't yet nine-thirty, or in desolate counterpoint it was even conceivable that the shop never had any other customers at all, it was all an arrangement awaiting the likes of himself. The girl got off her stool and went down an aisle. There seemed only enough air in the

7

place for the two of them. He became more aware of her, her dark sweep of hair, her heavy figure, her peasant blouse, she could have been twenty years old, she looked briefly his way and disappeared behind an old-fashioned door of pebbled glass in a wooden frame, so that he first imagined it must lead to a storeroom with perhaps a toilet at the back of it, but then, on account of the pebbled glass, that it might instead go to some sort of living space, a mom-and-pop operation, in this tiny building all of it contained. The records in the box were mostly Greek, Hadjidakis, Theodorakis, lefties defiant in this the evil time of the colonels' coup, but in there too he had found Leonard Cohen's first album, and he stared at the cover as if it were staring at him back. The spell was broken by the girl who had gone through the door. He could see her through the pebbled glass and he wondered at first what she could be doing there and then he couldn't quite tell but then he could. She was changing her clothes. She flung her arms up to get her peasant blouse free and her breasts were like a shadow theatre of breasts and then she was bent over like a Renoir with her breasts hanging down and her knees came high and her skirt came down and Leonard wondered if she could know what he could see. How could she not? Was it her first day on the job, had no one told her the dos and don'ts, was it the only place to change and so was she depending on the kindness of strangers to look away? Leonard could not look away. Five minutes hadn't passed since he first saw her yet he imagined the chance that she was putting on a show for him alone. And to what end, so that he would buy a book? She stretched her arms and in a way it was like a cartoon animal yawning, so that it might have been funny and sweet and he could see that too, but all he could really see were her breasts, which seemed to embody a heaviness of care, and then she was dressed in new clothes as if a film were running back to front and she came out and he looked away, to suggest his attention had never left the album cover of Leonard Norman Cohen, his droopy eyes, his melancholic danger. She was wearing a second peasant blouse now, its slivers of embroidery orange and green in substitution of the turquoise and blue. Seeing her dressed, his reason reasserted itself somewhat, the shop seemed warmer now so perhaps the first blouse had sweated through and she had changed so as not to face a day's worth of customers in sweaty clothes. But it was not even a quarter to ten, Leonard also considered, so how many blouses in a day would she wear, how many shadow plays perform? It was a mystery and he was still aroused and went to the desk and asked if she spoke English and if he could have a copy of the *Herald Tribune*. Yes, of course, she said, her voice husky and accented. There were *Herald Tribunes* behind the counter. But we only have it from two days ago, she said, so if you wait for tomorrow, you can have the new one. Leonard felt he should be a sport and buy the paper, even if it was days old, as if that would impress this woman whose breasts he had seen in shadow. It seemed to him that they had shared a secret. He bought the paper, asking her if she would pick the necessary coins out of his hand, which she did with the finesse of a small bird, her fingers nimble and precise in a way that her figure did not suggest, and he picked up his pack and his guitar and left, thinking only after he was gone that he should have asked her if she knew of a cheap place to stay.

But he found a place on his own and left his guitar and went to the beach where the Europeans went and he swam on his back in the buoyant sea. The *meltemi* returned and blew sand in people's faces and in their drinks and Leonard eyed other women's breasts with more than curiosity and rued

9

that he'd come to this beach at all, there being an obscure archeological site that he'd read about in a guide, where he might have climbed around in the heat with the snakes in the rocks and even have credited himself with some modicum of cultural taste, before his friends arrived and it was all-in on the last adolescent chase. Later he thought to return to the bookshop but there was an old man now at the desk who he could see from the road and he passed it by. He took a nap instead and in a furtive moment of the nap there seemed to be the pebbled glass, shadow play of an uncertain desire, then he awoke and got on a bus across the mountains to Panagia, a village on the other side, for he'd seen a poster in the town of lightning bolts and lit houses and it appeared that Panagia was to be electrified that night and it was something to do and he had nothing better. The colonels were pushing rural electrification that year. What was the point of democracy if you didn't have lights?

He arrived before dark but the colonels' men had no intention of throwing the switch set up in the village square before there were speeches and no intention of speeches until there was the drama of oncoming night and so the villagers sat gossiping in the arcs of chairs brought out from the cafés and the colonels' men stayed in their jeep, beneficent occupiers with an etiquette all their own. A few foreigners with cameras graced the edges. Wires crisscrossed the air to make the proper connections. At the end of one of the arcs of chairs, the girl from the bookshop sat alone. It took Leonard a few moments to notice her. She wore her outfit from work. She was somewhat looking around, she might have seen him or not. She stood out most of all because she was young and the villagers were all of them or most of them old, as if certain houses had emptied for the first time in awhile, putting a patina of rehabilitation on the square. Leonard went around to her. Her smile of recognition was thin and uncertain. From the shop, he said. Of course, she said. Is that seat…? he asked. Yes please, she said, and shifted her legs so he could get by. He brushed her knees without meaning to. When he was settled he had nothing to say that didn't sound as if he had reached into his back pocket for it. Her smile softened. How was your paper, she asked. I left it at the beach, he said. How was the beach, she asked. Boring, he said, then it sounded supercilious and too much like a boy, but he didn't know what to add to make it less so. It was minutes before they spoke again. Each looked around, two birds on different wires. The crowd thickened, the day faded and darkened, and two men in uniforms and one in an ill-fitting suit got out of the jeep. She glared at them with hatred.

Your friends, he said, and she glared at Leonard too until she was sure that he was joking. Then why did you come, he asked and she shrugged without an answer and by then it was night enough for the speeches. A priest came out from a café and joined the colonels' men and read a blessing. *May this gift from a far-seeing authority bring our community out of the darkness that the hippies elsewhere yet sleep in.* What did he say, Leonard asked when it was done and the girl translated and explained that on an island nearby there were hippies living in caves. She didn't approve of these, either, but there was something wistful in her saying it. The men in uniform took their cue from the priest, they praised themselves and their speeches were long and one of them in particular waved his arms the whole time as if calling on the air itself to be his witness. Then the man in the suit who was the mayor of Panagia gave thanks to God and to the armed services and threw the switch that was rigged to the podium and lights ticked on here and there, overhead and in the cafés, and a few in the arcs of chairs exclaimed their delight but the rest who had mostly seen whatever they were going to see in life clapped politely, the world continuing on its uncertain course whether they liked it or not. What's your name, Leonard asked the girl. Daphne, she said. Leonard, he said.

The bus left Panagia at nine and it was crowded with people who had come for the show and Leonard and Daphne sat together. There was nothing to it or it only seemed to happen, the logic of the other. He said he was from America and she said of course he was and for much of the way over the mountains it was she who talked and he who listened, as if to a tune he couldn't get out of his head, to the evils being done in his name, to Vietnam, to Johnson, to the CIA that had put the colonels in and he mustn't deny it because it had to be, there were a hundred proofs and the king had been in on it too, a puppet like the rest. There was an elation in her speech, a hurriedness, as if she had only a little time to get all of it in, as if the bus ride might be her only chance, and when he seemed stunned and distracted she demanded answers, and his answers weren't much, he was against the war, everybody was, things were bad, things were really bad, and she thought there was a dullness to his answers but then that she had put him on a spot and so she let it go. She had a round face and she was plump but not by much and her teeth were a little crooked in the way that American teeth were not. Coal-dark eyes, too, eyes of the Arabian Nights or anyway the album cover. When they arrived back in the port, he expected to shake her hand or whatever that would be and say good-night because that's how the native girls were, the Greeks weren't the Danes, or so the story went. And yet he thought of her through the pebbled glass.

Rather than say good-night they stood beside the bus and she asked would he like her to show him some things of the town and he said yes of course the way she had already once before said yes of course to him, with that air of certainty, that almost make-believe. So they walked the streets that he had walked earlier alone and as they walked a little slowly then slower still in a time warp of their own devising she told him stories that went from house to house and storefront to storefront, so that he would not think nothing ever happened in S., she said, there was the one-armed baker who lost his arm in the civil war, there was the woman who sold flowers by the fishermen's pier who fed so many cats she left no food for herself, there was the wife of the hardware guy Stavros who tried to poison Stavros's girlfriend, then everyone made up very well and seemed to be living happily ever after until the girlfriend tried to poison the wife. Then there were those who said her own father was communist when he wasn't. They said he was communist because he was a Jew, the old syllogism of the sacred and the scarred. It was when she said her father was a Jew that Leonard said his own whole name was Leonard Cohen, so there was that part of it settled. What Leonard did not express was his surprise, because he had been told there were no Jews left in Greece, that Hitler had got them all.

Again they tried or made the motions to say good-night. He no more knew her thoughts than he knew the name of her perfume, which was faint and came and went like the tides. They were in front of the bookshop now. She said to him that her house was in the back of it, that the door was in the alley. He said he would come to the shop in the morning. The way they talked to each other had become more jagged, as if each had things to say that couldn't quite hold a dialogue's straight line, thoughts stored up, thoughts rushing ahead, her English

that usually kept so easily up now showing Greek construc-
tions skeletally peeping through. She said if he would want to
she could show him one thing more.

So they walked out of the town on the main road and then
off the road and across a rocky field. Nor did they take each
other's hand once. They came out on the road again which
switched back as it rose. After that there were no more shortcuts and ahead of them was a black cliff to climb the back
of and then the unseen sea. Once more he followed her off
the road and they went up a steeper path that was rocky and
rooted and overgrown, single file on the narrow path in the
moonlight, until there was a wire fence and a gate. She opened
the dilapidated gate and they went through. Only then did
she declare it was her favorite place, as if she had wanted the
surprise, and he guessed what it was and said it, that it was
the ruin of Apollo Metameleia, which he mispronounced
badly but she half-laughed and corrected him and was happy
enough that he knew of it at all. It had been dug by museums
from Berlin and New York but the money had finished and
they hadn't found too much and it was abandoned now, she
said, though there was a local museum and in the museum
was some broken pottery. All he could see on the ground was
a slab of flat rock that shone dully in the moonlight as if
determined to give nothing away. She walked away from him
across several feet of uneven ground to the cliff's edge. He
came up behind her as she looked out. She seemed to feel
him coming and reached behind herself before he was there.
The water far below made a faint licking sound. Distantly on
the moon-dapple the ferry from S. was plying its way to the
next island on its route. It was running late as always. Strings
of white lights were strung on it like pearls, from its bow, to
its masts, to its stern. She remarked on them, she called them

that, strings of pearls, her strings of pearls. It wasn't so pretty up close, the ferry wasn't, Leonard said. Of course it wasn't, she said, a little impatiently but not too. Then some part of him touched some part of her, his hip or hers, his hand, her shoulder, so that he could feel the restless warmth that in the morning had sweated through her clothes. Neither of them could have said who turned first. They kissed because they were there or for a hundred other reasons. You can always come up with reasons, he thought, or she thought.

She brought him back by the hand to the slab of flat rock. It was cold when they lay on it and when she brought him on top of her it seemed to him almost as if she was protecting him from the cold, as if that was why. He felt her breasts and thought of the pebbled glass and didn't tell her what he had seen. Their lips were like little pillows, silk or velvet, touching almost too softly. His leg found space between hers and his knee touched through to the cold stone. And then what and then what and then what, and have you ever, she asked, for she knew or thought she knew that he was afraid, which he was. He touched her more, as if the fear would go away if he touched her more but when it didn't he told her that it wasn't quite true what she was thinking, and that he'd been with a prostitute once. She smiled then and said it would not count in her mind if it would not count in his, and he said that it wouldn't, so she took his fear in her hand which was soft and slightly plump and slid him towards her and they removed more clothes from each other so that she could finally say to him something like there were five billion people on the Earth in a rough amount so that in a rough amount this had happened at a minimum two and a half billion times before and his fear that she was holding she slipped inside her so that it would be gone forever.

3

Dear Leonard Cohen,

Everything with Daphne happened after I'd been to Hydra. I just want to make that clear. Hydra was first. One of the friends from Penn I was traveling with, Winston, his brother had been to Greece a couple of years before and he'd gone to Hydra and told him about it and so we went there.

I will tell you my first reaction: it was quaint enough. By that you'll infer I thought it was a little too quaint, which was true. No cars, all of that. I'd been writing a lot of songs on our trip. I'd heard it was also kind of an artists' colony on Hydra and I had a vague idea, with my new songs, that possibly I'd be a part of it. You see, yes, I was starting law school, and there was also of course the draft to contend with, but I still had big ambitions for myself. Escape the clutches of a gray world and all of that. I even thought I was good, undiscovered but good.

This was, as you know from my previous letter, before I'd even heard of you. That innocence was not to last long. We arrived on the fast boat from Athens and checked into the place where Winston's brother had stayed. I had my guitar of course and I believe it's accurate to say I was a kind of mascot to my friends. We would go places and I would play and sometimes it would even attract a little crowd. So we went to one of the cafés down by the water and I started to play and sing. I had all these new songs to sing. I had a terrible voice but figured that couldn't be held too much against

me because Bob Dylan had a terrible voice and look at him.
Dylan of course was already a star. Anyway. You can imagine.
I was a little bit shy, as well. Ambitious for myself but shy. Like
one of those actors who only lose their shyness on stage. Were you
like that? I'm guessing you were, though it's not something I can
remember ever reading.

Anyway after maybe fifteen, twenty minutes some people had
stopped to listen, who knows, they could have been people you
knew yourself, you probably did, your friends possibly, I mean
how many people were actually on Hydra at the time, Europeans
I mean, people from the north, Americans, tourists who forgot to
leave, that sort of person, but anyway they listened and pretty soon
somebody was buying rounds of ouzo. It was jovial, really, kind of
like hippie-days communal, everybody meeting everybody almost
on a lark, nobody working too hard at it, until people wanted
to know everybody else's names, like we should go around in a
circle or something. I could have said just Lenny but instead I
said Leonard Cohen. That really got things started. They thought
I was joking but I didn't get the joke. Then a guy I can remember
having a wandering eye who was probably stoned going in asked
was it some kind of trick I was playing. My friends hadn't heard
of you either up till then. By the time things got sorted out, that's
when I'd heard of you, of your existence, of your almost-fame,
of your being off in New York. All I could say was that I was
Leonard Cohen too. The people who'd been listening drifted away.

I never met Marianne. I never met anyone who specifically
said they knew you or you were their friend. But I was curious.
I felt my name had been stolen. Of course it hadn't been stolen,
but that's how it felt. I dismissed the chance that you had lapped
me, that whatever ambitions I had you were already far ahead
of, that I was always going to be the joke Leonard Cohen from
then on. Almost the opposite, I thought at first these people had

to be mistaken, that they were worshiping a false god so to speak, that whatever your achievements to date, once I got going, you'd be toast. Well, maybe not toast, I wouldn't have thought of the word toast, but you get the idea. I was the real Leonard Cohen, only undiscovered. It was reinforced by my feelings about Hydra, that it was too quaint. A great artist, a true rival, wouldn't live someplace too quaint.

All of that was before I heard your record. The pension where we were staying was posh enough to have a record player. Winston's brother Jamie wouldn't stay in no dump, I guess would have been the reason why. Anyway I splurged five dollars and found some sort of tourist shop that sold records, or at least they sold yours. Local hero. I remember they had your picture right next to your picture that was on the album cover, so they had your picture twice.

It's when I listened, back in the parlor of the pension, that I knew who was toast. I couldn't stop listening. I played each side three times. Your lyrics, your sentiments, all of it, so much stronger than mine, so much more mature, even your voice, which was even worse than mine but so much worse that it was better. Mine wasn't bad enough. Not nearly bad enough, not ruined enough by the world. And the album cover, with you looking sort of like me. That didn't help, either. In retrospect, it may have been why those people in the café thought I was trying to pull something off.

And "So Long, Marianne" especially. What did it mean? I couldn't even tell what it meant. All I knew was what they told me, that you were off in New York, making your way in the world, and Marianne was still somewhere on Hydra. I got out my own songs and reviewed them, compared them to what I had listened to. There was no real comparison. They were juvenile, unlived, derivative of things I couldn't even name. Yours were you, yours were life. I tore all of mine up, right then, that night, destroyed them, threw all the scraps in a bin. Now it's true and I'm sure you would agree that you can't really destroy a song once it's made, it lives in the memory of whoever made it, even in scraps. But I was so ashamed of myself, for my delusions, that I even willed myself to forget what I had done. Don't darken my door again, that sort of thing, dramatic, sophomoric, whatever. Start over, tabula rasa, but see what you're up against at least, see what a real Leonard Cohen can do. Only one song I saved, and I wrote it that night. Or it was a poem, really, if it was anything. It never had a melody.

11 Things You Can Do With a Guitar

Of course you can make
A lamp out of it. You can make
A lamp out of anything, they say
Out of hard feelings or an old sock
Or various everyday gizmos
Rusted Veg-O-Matics
Or a cock if it's put in formaldehyde
You can make a planter
Out of a guitar
Put the dirt in the hole
Put the seeds in the dirt
Et voilà, water well
Three you can smash a guitar
Over your best friend's head as if
The world were a vaudeville act or four
Make love with it
Using the long end as an aid
Guitar cases make excellent carry-ons
And you can have fun at the beach

Wooing the mermaids playing cowboy
That's seven play fruitcake with the devil
Take the whole thing and put it in a book
Like pressed leaves.
You can be buried with your guitar
Like a secret message to God
As to how you tried to live your life
Like a bandit, crazy and oddly
Pure of heart would be your claim
Eleven you can make a song
From its bitter ashes.

Yours,

Leonard

4

Dear Leonard,

   The next day I left Hydra, alone. I felt I should find an island that was less quaint. More authentic, if you will. I suppose, even then, in defeat, I was competing with you.

   Yours,

   Leonard

5

For four days they met each day after her work and climbed the rutted path to the moonlit slab that overlooked the sea, Apollo Metameleia, Apollo the Regretful One. She called him Apollo once or twice, a kind of second-language joke, when he looked regretful or whatever that was, the dreamy part, when their bodies were tired at last, when the worms would have their chance.

She never told him about the other lovers she had had and he never asked.

6

Something about the ancient adding machine in the shop, which had a lever that pulled hard and made a ringing sound, giving the pleasure of a slot machine without the chance. The day after they first made love Leonard came into the shop and she wasn't there and instead her father was at the desk, adding figures, pulling the lever, making the metallic ringing sound that Leonard remembered then from his grandfather who had a hardware store where as a child after the double feature he went on Saturday afternoons and his grandfather had had an adding machine that must have been the same or almost the same. Leonard loved the smell of the hardware store, sawdust and metal, sweet and hard, and now the smell of the bookstore, old paper and bindery glue and ink, sweet and soft.

Something about Daphne's father, too: Leonard ventured into the house in back of the shop once, she led him in, there was no one there but the housekeeper and themselves and in one small room with a narrow bed seemed as many books as in the shop, piled precariously or on shelves and stuffed around like makeshift insulation in the cracks, and when his eyes strayed to their spines the titles were all dusty German gothic, the greats her father would not give up on and never would, the war and the bitter all of it be damned, she said. Hofmannsthal, especially Hofmannsthal, she said, and Leonard thought again how much more of the world she knew than he did. A part Jewish, that too, she said, referring to Hofmannsthal whom he'd never heard of. Then the house-keeper wandered in and wandered out with half a flourish of a duster as if not to hide her nosing around and when she was gone Daphne said her name was Annie and she was her father's lover and had been his lover for years.

7

Dear Leonard,

Perhaps you've noticed, I've dropped the "Cohen" when I address you. In my last missive as well. I hope it doesn't presume too much. You seem more familiar to me now, more than through all the years when I never met you. And here's an odd thing I've thought about. Did you happen to belong to a high school fraternity? Mine had a branch in Montreal. Now that would be something, Lenny and Lenny, fraternity brothers. Though I don't think so. You were rich and I wasn't.

But I digress. We screwed and screwed some more. I can hardly remember now what that was like, the surprise and miracle and gratitude, all of that, so long ago. The way everything beyond the perimeter of our bodies was put aside for a little while. If we only keep doing this, things will turn out okay. Who needs the world? Well, I'm guessing now, trying to remember, being sentimental quite likely. But for sure we also talked. What a talker Daphne was. English as a second language? There were times I swore she could have had a secret Ph.D. Do you remember how Greeks speak English? They attack it a little bit.

She was Greek enough but of course Jewish too. In the winter they left the island and went north to Thessaloniki where the original of the bookstore had opened. Perhaps you know this, but I didn't, until she told me, there was a time when Thessaloniki was like the great Mediterranean city of the Jews. It was Salonica

29

then, part of the Ottoman Empire, and half its population was Jewish. After Greece got it back, after the first war, the Greeks were none too happy with the Jews' prominence and did their best to reduce it, and then of course the Germans took care of the rest. But Michail Sarfatty brought his family back there, after the DP camp, after a stay in Alexandria until Nasser booted them out of there too. Stubborn bastard, I guess. Reopened the shop. Daphne's mother kept it going in the summer while Michail came down to the island and the second shop and Annie. I took care not to inquire too closely about that arrangement. Let Daphne tell me if she wished, tell me whatever she wished.

But it was one topic she mostly avoided, the topic of her mother, or her mother's absence. About her father she was effusive, his politics, his time with the partisans in the civil war, his book-love, her fear that the military regime might come after him one day, exile him or shut him down or disappear him out of a helicopter. He had very much a quiet dignity, she said, which I can remember thinking was the kind of thing a daughter would say, the exact words a loyal daughter would say, or more precisely, what a daughter like Daphne would say.

What else, culled from her many words? Highlights of Daphne, ten quotes to remember her by? She seemed to think I could stop the Vietnam War all by myself. Hadjidakis over Theodorakis all days of the week. Why I should never get a haircut again. Americans and diets and the sadness of the world. The reason there were so few birds in Greece, because they were all eaten in the civil war. The Pill, thank the heavens for The Pill, The Pill had made it to Greece and even the colonels couldn't take it away. Her father favored Hofmannsthal but what about Joseph Roth, what about Stefan Zweig, names I'd again never heard of and even now have to look up online to be sure I get the spelling right. She had only finished high school. University was out of the question. The rest had come on its own.

We had more time to talk than to make love, in a practical sense, I mean. The shop was closed afternoons for the siesta, but there was no place to go to screw. She couldn't be seen to go to my room, nor me to hers. The slab was out of the question in broad daylight. We took walks, we bided our time, we sat in the cafés on the esplanade and talked as if we were in a movie with too much dialogue. Did I mention Daphne and cigarettes? I didn't smoke, never had. It was almost like that same movie with her, the way she butted out her stubby Greek cigarette when she had a particularly strong point to make.

Things we never talked about, aside from her mother: my seeing her through the pebbled glass; and you. Yes, you, yourself, the "real" Leonard Cohen, how I'd learned about you on Hydra, how I'd listened to your record so many times, and torn up my songs, and sworn defeat or revenge or victory or whatever it was I'd sworn to myself in my darkest corners. I didn't care to show Daphne my darkest corners, not yet anyway, not while we were having so much fun, not when it would be painful to drag them out, and possibly a disruption. Instead I painted her a rosier picture. I played her other people's songs on my guitar. Not yours, though. Never yours.

It all came out anyway, or something came out anyway. One afternoon I arrived at her house in back of the store because she wanted to introduce me, in a more formal way, to her father. He was short and bald and spectacled (have I mentioned this before?) with a mild handshake that was mostly fingers, and the eyes, now that he was observing me directly, I suppose of a skeptic. They regarded me for an extra second, but more than that I couldn't say, if he knew we were lovers, if he cared, if he'd seen it all before. It wasn't exactly the kind of question you ask your girlfriend's father, are you a communist at heart and do you believe in free love the way it's said that communists do, but it's what I wondered. As we chatted inconsequentially about, as I remember,

Akron, Ohio, where he had a brother-in-law and so Daphne an uncle of sorts, my eyes went over his shoulder to a record player in the corner. When I was left alone for a minute, Daphne making tea, her father returning to the shop, I went to the record player to have a look. I never asked myself really what I was looking for. Next to the record player was a short stack of records. I flicked casually through them. The third or fourth one down, after a Maria Callas and an ancient Furtwängler, was yours. Whatever I felt then I suppose I shouldn't have. I felt gamed. No, stronger than that. I felt betrayed.

Daphne came in with tea and a plate of little cookies too. We sat down and sipped the tea. We were like civilized people after all, our feral lovemaking the secret of the slab, the cliff, the sea. I suppose, as well, she was showing me something domestic. I said to her, after an unusual little while of quiet, as if the clicking of the teacups was saying something about us we hadn't known, that I saw in her records there was a Leonard Cohen. She was no dummy and took it for the beginning-of-an-accusation-or-an-argument-or-something that it was. She said nothing. She eyed me, really, with defiance, like what are you going to make of it, tell me, what?

I backed off a bit. Just wondering, I said.

Wondering what, she said.

Why you never told me you'd heard of him, when you heard my name, I said.

Aren't there a lot of Leonard Cohens, many Leonard Cohens, she said.

But with my guitar, I said. And being in Greece, I said.

Then her heart must have changed a little or she saw no reasonable way out, she being a person who reasoned her way through the world or thought she did, so then she said it was true it had occurred to her that our names were the same.

32

You never mentioned it, I would've thought you'd mention it, I said.

But you didn't mention it, you should have, it was necessary, if it meant so much to you, she said.

It would only have meant so much to me if you thought I was him, if you only went with me because I was him, I said.

But you looked a little like him, too, she said.

But I wasn't him, I said.

But I thought you were, yes, you're right, I did, I thought that, so go to hell, she said.

And when we first made love, you thought that too, you thought I was him then, I said.

Yes, yes, yes, I did, I thought you were him when we kissed and all of that, so leave me alone if that's what you want, just leave me alone, she said.

It wasn't a great scene. Looking back I can say that. Looking all the way back. The tea getting cold. I watched her until I couldn't, wondering when it was exactly that she realized I wasn't you, the exact moment, and was it on the slab, when I was in her arms. Then it occurred to me that that had to be the stupidest thing in the entire universe to wonder about, after I'd hurt her and for the first time. So then I told her about my envy of you, and my defeat, and tearing up my songs, all but one, which wasn't even a song. I confessed more than she did, was the way it turned out. First love, first fight, we would have screwed on the living room rug if Annie hadn't walked in then, Annie with her nose for whatever was going on. But we held on to whatever it was that had been let loose until dark and on the cliff that night we made love as if we meant it, nothing taken for granted, clinging a little, grasping a little, all in.

And after that night she called me "Leonard" less. Len-ny, she would call, with the accent on the second syllable. Len-ny this, Len-ny that, usually playful, once in a while exasperated or stern. "Leonard" more when there was a point to be made of it, a comparison or whatever, and it's possible she was anxious if she said it, uncertain what might come next, whether it might set off something strange in me that she'd rather not see. Though I don't remember specifically, I must have told her that I'd always been a Lenny and not a Len.

The next evening my friends from Penn arrived. We met them at the boat. Winston, Harv, Beeler. We took them out to dinner, showed them around a bit, checked them into the place I'd been staying. Daphne told me later she was certain Winston was CIA.

Yours,

Leonard

8

He explained to Daphne the unlikelihood of Winston being CIA. For one thing CIA didn't recruit much at Penn. CIA was more a Yale thing, maybe Princeton too, the old-line schools. Penn was old line but not the way that Yale and Princeton were. Yale, Princeton, WASPs. The subtleties escaped Daphne entirely, a world she painted in the brightest colors when she painted it at all. She was equally unimpressed by the fact that Winston was in ROTC. Leonard tried explaining the draft to her, selective service, 1A, 2S, 4F. All she hoped was that he would stay out of it and he said there was a chance he could and a chance he couldn't and it would depend on whether his right leg was enough shorter than his left. She offered to cut off an extra piece of it just in case. As for Harv, he was going to med school which would keep him out of it and Beeler was teaching in a poverty program which would keep him out as well but Winston was their sacrificial goat, he was in ROTC which meant he was going to Vietnam for sure. She nodded, a little dazed with too much information, too many initials, and repeated her belief that Winston was CIA, he just looked it, the blond look and all of it.

Once his friends arrived, Leonard began to spend time with them in the hours that Daphne spent in the shop. They gave him the conventional sort of shit for going with a townie, for having a girlfriend at all. What kind of way was that to spend the summer of love? None of them suspected it was his first. If they had known, they might have been less concerned or more, the wry calculations of dozy afternoons. In all events she was plump and the girls they were looking for were not. And *zaftig* entered the conversation a couple of times, Winston showing he could keep up with his Yiddish even if it sounded restless and exotic in his mouth. The others had been in Athens awaiting cash infusions from their respective fathers. Leonard had had no such cash infusion to expect. Now they were hoping S. would be the party-and-beach paradise that Beeler had heard about on a tipsy night in the Plaka but if it wasn't then it would be on to the next. Winston was headed soon for trouble and the rest were getting on with their lives and the wisdom was that there was no time to waste.

If anybody had asked, Leonard might have dissented, but no one asked. They wondered, though, what had happened to all his songs. It was like a blacklist had been declared in Leonard's mind and he'd hidden them all away in a drawer for a better day, or some invisible censor had declared them obscene. When he played his guitar now, if he played it at all, the words and melodies were not his own. He didn't care for Dylan much, but he played him now. And Joni Mitchell had just appeared and he tried out *Song to a Seagull*. But what had happened to *their* Leonard Cohen? Predictably they blamed Daphne for the transformation more than the guy with the same name who had run away from Hydra to New York.

Like a man trying to escape a labyrinth, going this way then that, doubling back around, Leonard showed Daphne his one piece of work, his song without a melody. She told him it didn't sound like him while he assured her that it did. He became moody around her, as if to punish her for too much truth. And it wasn't an act, or if it was, the act was a secret even from himself. His worlds were either colliding or drifting apart, tectonic plates without anchors. He wished his friends had never showed up, then the next minute was so glad they had that if they had tied him to a mast he would have thanked them with bleats of joy. In the mornings they all went to the tourists' beach, the one he'd never been to with Daphne, and they swam there and joked and looked at the many bodies of women and nothing much happened but it was something to do.

But when it was evening Leonard snuck away, and during the siesta hours too. He was really gone and it was weird, they thought, Lenny was acting too weird.

Finally of another evening it seemed to him there was nothing more he could say to Daphne, not a single word being both straight enough and clean enough. His tongue was metallic. They were standing again at the edge where the ruin met the sky that had been the most glorious outpost of his world and it had all become too familiar. Was the night demanding answers of him? They weren't quite touching, looking out, the ferry, the midnight sea.

Then something, the dark or the ferry or the insistent lapping of the water or *some*thing, got him to give up the last secret he held close, the last one anyway he knew enough to put a name to, and he played it down when he told her because it was too shameful or embarrassing not to, and he was afraid also that it could be a brag. You know what I want to do with my life? All I want to do with my life. This would be enough. I want to write one song that's as good as one of Leonard Cohen's.

She laughed then but it wasn't to be mean. She thought it was funny in a touching way or touching in a funny way, or heartbreaking, or only something to break the ice. For he had become like ice.

She thought to say, but you *are* Leonard Cohen, but she didn't.

She thought to say, which song of his, because he's written quite a lot of them and it seems some are very much better than the others, but she didn't say that either.

Nor did she say, when she thought to say it, okay, good, *kala*, get to work, but if you don't do it or can't do it there are still a million things you can do, the world is very damaged, there's much room.

Then in place of words she thought to take his hand and lead him to the slab with the hope that he would soon forget, but she knew that she herself would not soon forget, and if she would not, how could he?

So they stood there looking out and she read his doubts more deeply and at last she said, go, you should go. You have to. Of course.

Go where? he said.

To your song, she said.

What a crazy thing to say. Each of them had a version of that thought. She kept her eyes on the horizon as if it were seasickness she was trying to stop.

Then he took her hand rather than the other way around and led her to the ground the way she had often led him and in the middle of their two becoming one in the only way they knew how she cried I'm sorry, I'm sorry, I'm sorry, forgive me for thinking you were him, for wanting you to be him, so that Leonard felt something at last, anything at last, and he licked her moist eyes dry, then they went on with it.

9

Dear Leonard,

You of all people would know what she meant by "your song." I had told her my secret wish and her mind had run with it. And so what was hiding in the plain sight of it all was a truth I could hardly avoid. I might love her or I might not, but if I stayed with her I would have nothing to write about. I would only have lived "so far."

Or that was one possibility, one theory of the case, the other being that she was my "soulmate," to use the terminology of the times, and in her, in her speech, in her body, in her surprises, I would find everything, even myself. I wasn't sure. I thought it was something I should be sure about, you don't just go guessing about such things, you don't just leave it to your mind. Another way of saying it, I suppose, is that I knew nothing about love. How could I? Touch it? Feel it? "This can't be love, I feel so well." That old line, too. Unless I "lived," I was never going to know.

And I had this other dreary little thought as well. I was starting law school in a month. Making a go of it in dreary student housing in Philadelphia. Me off to the library. What would Daphne do? Go off to protest the war? Stay home and iron the clothes? That tiny apartment. And what if I did wind up drafted? It felt almost like a solution.

Her mind of course had raced ahead of me. Of course I would leave. Summer romance, what do you expect? She'd been to the movies more than I had.

And yet she had hopes, stored up, which is what moved me most and finally, the kid who bled stones, when the next morning after she told me I needed to go find "my song," I went to the bookshop and saw, by the old adding machine, an envelope that said, in the little bit of Greek lettering I could decipher, all caps thankfully, AMEPIKH. I asked her what it was. She said it was nothing. I asked her if I could see it and reached out my hand because it said America after all and so it must have to do with me. She took my wrist to stop my reach but not before I lifted it just a bit, enough to know there was money inside. Coins, some bills. She was saving up for a plane ticket. She denied it. She put the envelope away in a drawer and as she did so it tinkled, or whatever you say, the sound of money, but not just any money, coins, the littlest money, as if she were saving every bit. Tears, then, but they weren't hers. She must have been counting up how much she had when I walked in.

Yours,

Leonard

10

Dear Leonard,

You know the way in the Middle Ages they used to decide trials by dunking somebody in water and if they sank or floated decided whether they were innocent or done for? My trial, I decided, was whether I had a wonderful song to write. And I didn't. At that moment I didn't have any song at all. I was still struck mute from comparison to you, who had lived, who <u>was</u> living, who seemed like he wasn't going to stop. "So Long, Marianne." If I left her, wouldn't the leaving be what I had to write about?

Or could I write my own song which would be about leaving but not actually leave? Why couldn't I tell a lie? It was my own song, why couldn't I tell all the lies I wanted, or I could write about telling the lies, or I could write about wondering whether I could tell the lies and get away with it, wondering whether the lies would be any good? Or I could write about the dreary room in Philadelphia that awaited us, but why would I bother, why trouble the world with it, and wouldn't writing bitter lies be worse than leaving? I felt lapped all over again.

You were the example in my mind. A test case. You must already have been more than that in Daphne's. I began imagining she had studied you more than she let on. Studied you, even, to get more truth about me, or was it just the other way, was it I who was the test case for some imaginary fixed star of you?

I still thought of the pebbled glass. More often now I thought it must have been a trick, a country-girl seduction. I thought so because hadn't she deceived me about her Leonard Cohen record, about having confused me with you? Fool me once, shame on you, fool me twice, shame on me, that old cruel, wicked saw of the fallen.

Yours,

Leonard

11

Dear Leonard,

My friends meanwhile were getting anxious to leave S. And I could see their point. As a party and beach paradise it wasn't quite ideal. Their luck with finding Scandinavian girls of a certain shape and disposition hadn't been that great. I felt their tug, their urgency, as if anyone could say it was the most superficial thing in the world but what if it wasn't? The chorus in Guys & Dolls singing love is the thing that has licked 'em and it looks like Nathan's just another victim. Another song I remembered then.

Winston, Harv, and Beeler were my way out. They were an excuse.

And was I entirely free of what to avoid an argument let's just call their youthful high spirits? Not really. Not entirely. Daphne's look. If I could have imagined previously who I would have fallen for, it would not have been her. Zaftig, not for me. Was I simply a captive of her body? Once more, men of a five-and-dime Odyssey, tie me to your mast.

I was fighting off a cloudiness, a kind of heaviness it felt like as well, as if it might drag me down to a sleep from which I would never wake up.

Of course she must have known that too. Seen it in my fear, or in a hundred other ways, all invisible to me.

Yours,

Leonard

12

Dear Leonard,

The temple of Apollo Metameleia, the sad little abandoned ruin. My friends weren't that interested in seeing it. I was. I suppose that was a difference.

Yours,

Leonard

13

Dear Leonard,

Metameleia, the regretful one. But what did Apollo have to be regretful about?

Yours,

Leonard

14

Dear Leonard,

And while we're on the subject of the ancients, of the old-timers. What about competition itself, the race of life I seemed to have entered myself in? Is it a good and natural thing or a sin? Greco-Roman, Judeo-Christian, all those hyphens on and on, how did people come up with those hyphens anyway? Or maybe in that monastery on Mount Baldy they convinced you it was all an illusion so do whatever you must but try not to fool yourself while you're doing it. Seems like I've read that book, too. I would be grateful for your opinion. I would be grateful if you ever figured that one out.

Yours,

Leonard

15

Dear Leonard,

I promised her I would return. I would leave for a week with my friends but then I would be back. You won't, she said. You're my Leonard Cohen, she said, emphatically.

I even said I would leave my guitar, if she didn't believe me, as a guarantee. But she wouldn't have it.

Yours,

Leonard

16

The museum was in a concrete block of two rooms that huddled on the outskirts of the town like something left over from a war. Leonard found it with a map. No other tourist bothered to visit it that morning so that it had the aspect of a fool's errand, but he found it cooler inside than it appeared, a respite, a retreat. There were glass display cases that could as easily have held butterflies stuck with pins and in each room there was a bench in the middle. He examined the contents of the display cases in turn, the fragments of a krater, one pot put badly back together, portions of necklaces, shards of marble, bits of broken column. If there had been anything good, it would now have been in Berlin or New York.

Leonard sat on the bench in the second room and while it may have appeared he was trying to think, he was in reality trying exactly not to think but rather to feel, and he was having not an easy time of it. In the second room was a drawing depicting what the god might have looked like, peering from an inner sanctum. He wore a laurel wreath and he held his lyre. Leonard couldn't really tell if he looked regretful or not. He had that lofty look, that fuck-you-can't-you-tell-I'm-a-god look.

Then a bit of impatience seeped in. How long had he been sitting? He felt he had cast himself into a bad play, the insincere seeker. The seeker who didn't even know what he was seeking. Tell me about love, Apollo. Apollo predictably had nothing to say. The laurel wreath, significant, don't make me laugh, Leonard thought. And the silence of the god's lyre, his fingers not even touching the strings. Play me a song about love, Apollo.

Then the caretaker of the museum, a woman in black who wore her disposition as obscurely as her age, entered and said something to him in Greek. Leonard looked at her quizzically. She carried a bucket in one hand and gesticulated with the other. Get up, get up, her hand gestures said, and so he did. Then she gave him a toothless smile and splashed whatever was in her bucket on the bench and withdrew a rag from her black apron and wiped it dry. When she was done, she motioned that he could sit again. He grimaced and remained standing. He thought of Daphne's body, its oozy warmth, and the scent of her, sweaty and giving. Best to be silent. Best not to hope nor to dream. The caretaker left the room. Leonard checked his watch, a reflex, a habit, as if he were checking on the progress of the world in his absence.

17

Dear Leonard,

It was going to be the Friday night boat. On Thursday after-noon, in the siesta hours, we had it out again. I insisted I would be back in a week. I had checked the ferry schedules. There would be a return boat the following Friday. This was on the esplanade that we talked, in the café we always went to, and Daphne kept telling me to keep my voice down. But I thought I was *keeping it down. It was possible she was only trying to change the subject when she said it, but change the subject to what? It was easier for her to say her mind than for me, because she knew her mind.*

She said again that I would not be back, and it was only natural, she said.

Of course I would be back, I said.

Then I would not be, then I would be, it ping-ponged back and forth, until finally I said "I love you" because I really did intend to be back and how else would I win the argument, and whether I meant it or not, and whether she knew whether I meant it or not, and whether I knew if she knew whether I meant it or not, it all went by.

What would Leonard Cohen do, she said.

Which Leonard Cohen are you referring to, I said.

You know which is the one, she said, and if I didn't shut up right then she would sing "So Long, Marianne" to me, and did I want that or didn't I? Very loud in public, just like that, where

55

everybody could be hearing, very embarrassing, Len-ny, very much so. Then her hearty laugh, her cackle that broke my heart, such that I remembered I had just said "I love you" and now I believed it all. Then I thought again of the tiny apartment in Philadelphia we would have and how it would all come crashing down.

I know what you're thinking now, she said.

I'm thinking about that money you're saving up for America, the money in the envelope, I said.

Do you know if that's for you, she said.

Wasn't it, I said.

It could be for Chicago, it could be for Boston, it could be Akron, Ohio, she said.

Were you invited to Akron, Ohio, I said.

It doesn't matter, it's the principle, she said.

And it was true. Daphne had principles. She adhered to principles. How selfless, how unbelievable, now she called on art to prove it once and for all. You'll write about leaving me, she said. Wonderful songs about leaving me.

Don't say that, I said.

Why not if it's the truth, she said.

I'll be back in a week, I said.

Then, as if to nail her point to the wall, as if having the illustrious Leonard Cohen in her corner wasn't enough for her, she started quoting Kierkegaard of all people. It wasn't going to do much for me, who was aware of the name and little more, an answer in some game I was never good at, but she may have said it for herself, to convince herself.

The line was this. Couldn't fault her for not being in point. "I see that the notion of my existence founders over this young girl, ergo the young girl must vanish."

Maybe she didn't have the words exactly, but close, close enough.

She may even have been feeling some bitter triumph then. The triumph over your own feelings, is there a more bitter triumph than that?

Fuck all, Leonard. I started thinking it was possible she just wanted me to leave, period, and this was her clever way out, art over life. But I didn't really believe that either.

Yours,

Leonard

18

How ordinary their lovemaking was that night, as if, if they acted like nothing was about to change, then it wouldn't. The magic of bodies, to pretend, to make do. It was one thing they seemed to agree on, that time itself can be made to expand or contract. A day was like a universe. She had brought a blanket with them. They had never had a blanket before. They lay on their backs and watched the moon. Daphne told him what its trajectory would be. Otherwise they spoke very little.

The next morning he went early to the shop but she wasn't there. Her father was cutting the pages of a book with a card. Scarcely looking up, he said to Leonard to check the quay, but she wasn't there either. Then he walked around the town as you might look for a lost cat, asking shopkeepers, but none had seen her.

He went back to the pension, as if surely she would stop by if he showed no unease and patiently waited or even better if he would sit there in the garden with his guitar because it was past checkout now. The others had packed their belongings too and gone to the beach for a last swim. In the garden with his guitar perhaps he would pluck out a new song, something to show her, something to prove whatever needed to be proved. It had been Leonard's experience that if you wished for more than one thing then the chances of at least one of them happening were improved, it seemed no more than a mathematical formula, a simple calculation of the odds, a way to hedge every bet, but neither Daphne nor a song came.

Then it was the afternoon and he went back to the shop and then to the house in back of it in the alley, where Annie acted as if he were already gone, which suggested to Leonard the conversations that might have been had in which he was not the hero.

Until then he had avoided the rutted path to the cliff, out of a feeling that if she had gone there she would take it badly to be disturbed, but now he climbed the path for the first time alone and in daylight and was shocked by the sweeping views, the bank calendar views, as if what he'd only ever seen at night had a second life. It took an hour up and back and he was aware now of time's passing, but she wasn't there either.

He tried to put himself in her mind. There were only so many places she could be. She had to be hiding or running or afraid but if he could only find her he would kiss her tears, because of course there would be tears. How little he knew and how deeply he wished, in these hours, that he knew a little more. He was the supplicant, not the hero, now. But still he felt that she would not let him leave without saying good-bye. Her slow, careful, observant inwardness, her way of never missing a thing: they would not allow it. She would show up at the boat. She would wave. He felt helpless, as if it were he who should be the one to be sure to say good-bye.

At seven the others picked up their belongings and headed down to where the *caique* would take them out and he went with them. Beeler asked him where Daphne was, he called her by her name, not "your girlfriend" or "your girl" or "your townie" or any of those in descending order of civility or luck. Leonard said they had already said their good-byes but the others could see him looking around. The ferry came around the head of land from the north and blew its horn which was the sign for the *caique* to load up. Out beyond the head, the *meltemi* was again blowing strongly. It would be a rough passage, the fishermen said, and laughed and made gestures and pantomimed people throwing up. The friends clambered aboard the *caique* and Leonard still looked around, up and down the quay. He felt the horn might bring her out, a last call.

From the deck of the ferry the town seemed to Leonard to be ignoring its resident's rude behavior. It went about its business as though nothing of consequence had happened at all. Lights twinkled on, seaside *tavernas* filled, the whole white arc of buildings reached around as if to embrace the evening as it had embraced ten thousand evenings before. Leonard waved uncertainly once or twice just in case but there was no one waving back. Where there was no one he imagined a conversation. He said to no one "I don't desire you less" and no one said to him "But you desire the world more."

19

Dear Leonard,

My friends thought they had died and gone to heaven. That old phrase. The beaches, the all-nighters, the girls with names like Erika or Annika, all the ones with ks in their names, on the beaches and in the clubs. Though there weren't so many clubs on Ios then. Mostly we stayed on the beach, making fires, me playing my guitar. Winston got lucky a lot, taking pains not to mention to the girls that he would soon be a second lieutenant in Vietnam. Harv and Beeler each had their moments as well. Happier than pigs in shit, another thing they said or thought. Though Beeler, ever the fair-minded one, was quick to point out the insult to the pigs. And me? I was the mascot again, the background music, the piano player in Casablanca or one of those. I had for the moment lost my taste for boys' adventuring. It wasn't for me, it had never been, I thought, though I was happy enough to be with my friends. I can't say that I missed Daphne then. I thought about her all the time, made comparisons and wondered, but I can't say I missed her. What was there really to miss if I would see her in a week?

There was one incident, if that's the word for it. One chance that came my way. I think her name was Anja, no, bullshit, I <u>know</u> her name was Anja, can't get out of that one so easily by pretending to forget her name. Anja seemed to take a liking to how I played the guitar. Why does that remind me of the old Hollywood

63

joke, the starlet dumb enough to fuck the writer? Anyway Anja wasn't a starlet, she was from Helsinki, and all I can remember really about her were her freckles and her teardrop face and up the beach somewhere away from the fire we'd made and after I'd kissed her awhile and pawed her a bit, she took off her shorts and I promptly came on her stomach or her thighs or somewhere that wasn't intended and the last thing I remember is soon afterwards her walking up the beach away from me with her shorts in her hand. So these things happen, as they say, and what do they mean if anything.

My revenge, always my revenge, was to write songs. Though I could never have said who my revenge was against. But it got me going at least. We were living on the beach then. It seemed de rigueur in a weird way, following the fashion, when in Rome et cetera, so during the day I would retreat to the nearest taverna, which was a place just off the beach with a little shade and a few uneven chairs that sold orange drink and Fix beer and souvlakia. Out of the sun and the boring chase, I scribbled in a small student's pad. Once I got going, I kept going, three, ten, twenty songs, plus jots for what the melodies would be. I didn't ask myself if they were any good. They were mostly about Daphne, some aspect or other of her, but they weren't about leaving her because in my mind I hadn't left her. Wrestling with the truth again, not coming out on top. One song was about coming back to her. Another was about her not saying good-bye. I wrote her a postcard and then I wrote a song about writing her a postcard. Then I wrote a song about the postcard never arriving.

I didn't play any of those songs at night on the beach. I was an entertainer of sorts. I played Dylan, I played Joni and Joanie, a little Beatles of the more balladic sort, and yes, I tried a song or two of yours, just to see if I could, just to see if envy and depression would rise up and get me, which they did. Winston provided commentary, "our" Leonard Cohen versus the "real" Leonard Cohen. It got a few puzzled laughs from the girls when it was explained to them.

My friends were perfectly happy to spend the rest of their vacation days on Ios. The day for my boat back to S. arrived. It was a real parting and we knew it. I was the only one of us going back to Philadelphia in the fall. Beeler's grade school was in Meridian, Mississippi. Harv's med school was in Iowa. And Winston was due to report in September at Ft. Ord in California. I felt a little like a traitor, leaving before the last minute. What kind of party would it be back in Athens without Lenny? Who'd play the mournful fucking guitar shit? Who'd have the melody for the big drunk? Instead I hugged Winston on the beach, more hippie-ish than any of us were. But who knew, who could say, what was just around the corner? It was a rough world out there. As for the others, fuck 'em. See you around, Beels. Fuck yourself, Harv. A few more sort-of hugs. And don't put your dick in any hairy Greek armpits. That was Winston, as I recall, to me. Not quite in point but close enough. They wished me well with Daphne, and whether they meant it or not or believed it or not, we all knew it was the thing to say.

I felt, when I found Daphne, I would have a nice haul of songs to show her. Beyond that, I couldn't quite imagine.

Yours,

Leonard

20

His plan had been to go to the alley and under her window strum his guitar just a little, a joking-around Romeo, but the ferry arrived after midnight and he knew he could not strum softly enough and there seemed no point to waking up the world. Besides, if his postcard had arrived she might have met him at the boat, she might have been there even if she was mad, even if she was only curious, but she wasn't there. He wondered if the postcard had arrived, he tried to imagine the efficiency of the Greek mail. He scanned the esplanade and the cafés and walked a little around the town, seeing no one he knew at all, then went to his old room, a little disappointed, a little put out, as if where were the girls waving handkerchiefs or scarves to welcome him home or the brass band. The town seemed quiet. New tourists had arrived, strangers, wandering around. He felt passé and went to sleep.

In the morning the shop was closed. This seemed odd. Leonard tried to remember if it was Sunday. And even if it was. A CLOSED sign hung on the door, abrupt, definitive, one side English, one side Greek. Maybe she had overslept, maybe someone had the flu, he wondered, and went round to the alley. But when he knocked, no one came to the door. He knocked louder, to show he meant business or to plead. He wondered if they were all conspiring against him, peeking from behind a curtain, whispering to each other to stay away. Now he came around again to the front of the shop, to leave a note, to let

67

her know, and in the little time he was gone someone had left a small bouquet of white carnations on the door, their stems threaded through the CLOSED sign. He knew the flowers meant nothing good. Illness, sudden departures, death. He at once tried to estimate her father's age and to remember if in his appearance there had seemed anything amiss.

Some things it doesn't matter if you saw them coming or not. Leonard looked up and down the street of shops for anyone to ask. Yet he didn't know even what his question would be. What was in his mind and what was in the world became confused, intertwined. The butcher, the baker, the candlestick maker. He felt a little bit blind. The remorseless sunlight, the whiteness of the houses, all seemed to be conspiring against him. He yearned to see Daphne. He wished she would protect him even as he sensed that it was she who needed protection. And he would provide it, unstintingly. Did any of this make sense? Of course, of course, find her, find out what's going on. Or was it only a national holiday? The simplest explanation of all, the likeliest explanation. He checked to see if the bank was open. People were walking in and out. He told himself to calm down. And when he calmed down, there was Stavros the hardware guy in front of his shop, putting out some flower pots and brooms. No poisonings in the family today, Stavros? Everything *andaxi* on the home front?

Leonard had spoken to Stavros once before, when he'd gone in with Daphne to buy a roll of tape. Now Stavros saw him coming and turned away and Leonard thought if even Stavros turns away that can't be good either.

Stavros, *parakalo*, Daphne, Leonard said while Stavros went about his business, fussing with his brooms.

Parakalo, please, Leonard said again and Stavros made a

show of embarrassing him, arranging his brooms with military precision against the glass, nothing in the world being more important than their proper order, a strong military, a strong state, a strong hardware store.

Leonard came closer to Stavros, in the doorway of the shop, and raised his voice the way a man who seldom raises his voice would raise it, with all the fear locked inside, so that what came out sounded something like lead. *Pou eeneh* Daphne, where is Daphne?

It was then that Stavros cursed him, the ancient curse of five fingers, pushed towards Leonard's face as though to say don't darken my door, and Leonard shrank back a little and exclaimed in a voice that had already guessed too much, *giati, giati*, why?

The girlfriend, the poisoner, must have heard some of it or seen it and came out of the hardware store and said only, Daphne *kaput*, and made a gesture like a bird or a plane falling out of the sky, a swooping arc with her whole arm.

Leonard fell back. Later he would think is there another word for death uglier than *kaput*, but for the moment he only staggered and tried to disbelieve. If you're young enough and lucky enough to have been close to death only a little, to have only brushed it by or seen it on an indistinct horizon, you might be forgiven for disbelieving, for trying to find another way out, but soon he stopped trying.

There was no pity in the girlfriend's voice nor in Stavros's stare. Leonard asked them nothing more and backed away and again there was the unforgiving sunlight, everywhere unforgiving sunlight, as if in cahoots with the others. When it goes wrong, it all goes wrong.

He went back to the bookshop door. He stared at the white carnations. He peered into the dimness of the shop, a welcoming darkness. The books piled high, the adding machine, then a view dimly to the back of the shop and the door with pebbled glass.

Wishing to turn back the days. And who could he speak to? And where was the father? He would wait outside their door. He would wait and wait. But after an hour a stranger came by and placed more flowers. He was middle-aged with a receded hairline and he looked with the flowers in his hand like a suitor. More eyes dark with grief. The man spoke no English but when Leonard pointed through the door and said *kyrios*, mister, and *pateras*, Daphne *pateras*, the mourner who looked like a suitor said *Saloniki*, so that part of it was solved.

Then he walked the streets of the town with his head down, staring at the white between the pavers as if he were mapping out worlds, better worlds. When he found he was going around more or less in circles, when he had come upon no familiar face, he went back to his room and lay on his bed. At least it was dark. The heat of the day was up and the ceiling fan above the bed turned languidly to little effect. He studied it as if it were a rare insect. One of the bolts holding it to the ceiling was loosened, so that the fan hung at a drooping angle, by only an inch or two but enough so that he could imagine at any minute it might come loose altogether, death by renegade ceiling fan, sliced and diced Leonard, a kind of solution. He slept a little while. He longed to dream.

He was awakened by a light knocking on his door. Who is it? he called. Is it okay, I turn down bed, the woman's voice called back, and Leonard knew at once that although he couldn't find a soul to speak English, a soul had found him. He told her please come in. He got off the bed so that she could do what had to be done. The day had lost its insistent luster. He must have slept longer than he thought.

He watched her do her little chore. She was an older woman he couldn't remember from before. Women in black dresses, the invisible ones. Perhaps she was the owner's mother. You speak English, he finally said.

Liga, a little, *liga anglika*, she said, but really it was more than a little and who could say from where.

Could I ask you something, Leonard said.

Of course, she said, and Leonard liked the way she said it, of course instead of yes, the way Daphne always said it, in that attacking way.

Daphne Sarfatty, do you know her, he said.

Yes, she said and looked more carefully at him.

Is it true, is she dead, he said.

Yes, true, she said, it is true.

When, he said.

Last week, she said.

Do you know which day, he said, and the woman tried to think and counted back.

Friday, he asked.

Yes Friday, she said.

At night, he asked.

Yes night, she said.

And how, he asked.

Off the mountain, she said.

She fell, he said.

She fell, she said.

There were more details then, a few, the story was out there, people had wondered, all were shocked. So terrible, so young.

And to paraphrase, to fill in the pidgin blanks until enough of it was there: it must have been sometime around or after midnight because people saw her wandering a little time before, and they thought it was odd, she looked a little odd,

71

but not so much, people said, to be upset about, but of course they would say that later, of course they would, if they saw her so odd and did nothing. The next day the son of one of the fishermen was in his father's boat out to sea but not too far and saw a bright patch on the shore which was very odd so that he came in and the bright patch was the clothing, her blouse, and there she was, on the rocks, below the mountain.

Was this below where the temple was, Leonard asked, and she didn't seem to know the temple, so he said the ruins, the ruins, and she said yes, below the ruins.

He waited until it was dark. They had always gone up by moonlight and the moonlight had always been enough. Where the path began at the Panagia road there were more flowers, as if it had been a roadside accident, one of those that happened so frequently in 1968 that there was a national campaign to teach people how to drive better. And, oddly, as well, there was a cross. He climbed the rutted path to see for himself but it was a path that at night he had only ever taken with her and as he climbed he asked himself what it was that he expected to see. He thought of the other Leonard Cohen then, the "real" Leonard Cohen, and how he would have liked to ask him if there were two kinds of loneliness, and in one of them there were people running around and buses and trains and laughter and other signs of life like donkey shit on the path in front of you and in the other you were alone in the universe.

But he knew it was not a question, and that was the whole problem. Or was it the other way around, he also wondered, was it when there's donkey shit on the path in front of you that you're really and truly and utterly alone? Leonard had thought he was growing up. He had thought he was becoming more like the "real" Leonard Cohen. How he hated himself then, climbing up that path. Where was she? Nowhere at all.

When he reached the top and the ruins, he noticed something quite odd, quite unbelievable really. By the slab where they had made love, at the very edge of the cliff, a young tree was growing. It had not been there before. Leonard felt certain he would have seen it if it had been there before. There hadn't been a tree in sight before. It was all scrub and rock and in August even the wildflowers that squeezed their life out of the cracks in the rocks had died.

In the moonlight the tree's leaves shone darkest green, the green most akin to black. He had no idea what sort of tree it was, its name, its provenance, its likelihood to be found in a high place in Greece. All he knew was that it had not been there before.

Could someone have planted it in the hard and pebbled ground? There was no sign of digging, no little piles of dirt like ant hills around.

Could a tree grow so fast? Leonard didn't think so, though he knew there were weeds that grew fast, you could go to sleep and in the blink of an eye they were three feet high. He'd had a grandmother whose life went by in a postage-stamp garden complaining of those.

Then he was thinking of Daphne again. He stood next to the tree with his toes over the cliff's edge so that he could look at the lapping water down a thousand feet or whatever it was and wonder. The moonlight on the water seemed to be playing a game, hide-and-seek or catch-me-if-you-can. He had the thought, for just a moment or maybe two, how delightful it would be to join the moonlight in its game. Then he heard Daphne's voice. *Len-ny, Len-ny,* the voice said, the way Daphne so often said *Len-ny,* with the accent on the second syllable, teasing, chiding, brimming over with life. He turned and heard *Len-ny* again. The voice was coming from the tree.

21

Dear Leonard,

When I heard Daphne's voice coming from the tree, my first reaction was to doubt my senses and the second was to doubt my sanity. There was the added, intensifying factor that I felt certain the tree had not been there before. That certainty began to erode. I was notorious for never having noticed much about nature. How could I be so sure of something I'd never seen before? I stared at what really was little more than a sapling. Seeds blow from everywhere, I thought. The meltemi was blowing, albeit lightly. Couldn't the sound of the wind have produced a "Len-ny" for my eager ears? And why shouldn't I be insane with grief?

I said something idiotic. It had to sound idiotic, released into the air. Did you say something, I said. A cosmic joke if there ever was one, but it's what I said. Did you say something. And I added, with a question mark, Daphne? As if things would be straightened out if she identified herself. I was terrified. I could barely move. The tree said nothing more.

A man with his faculties more stable might have stuck to something closer to my first reaction and concluded simply that he had made a mistake. The episode would have passed. But I longed to hear her voice. If it was only the wind passing through the little tree that composed it, still I longed to hear it. Composed out of my own longing, that too. Daphne, I said again, Daphne, please, speak to me.

But she had had her say. And so had I. I backed away to the slab, as if the stone under my feet would give me stability. I stared at the little tree. I prayed that Daphne was somehow alive, though I didn't know much about prayer. I regretted everything that I had done and not done.

Sorry. That was one thing more I said. Old ineffectual sorry, that fills in the space where there's nothing. Then I stumbled down the path, away from all of it. Who did I think I was speaking to then? The answer's obvious, I guess. Or is it? Was I only speaking to myself?

When I got back to my room, it was as though I remembered an earlier instinct, as though I'd been right about something the first time, and why had I ever doubted myself? Déjà vu all over again, a command performance, I took every scrap of paper where in my mini-comeback I'd written a song or an idea for a song or a snatch of melody and tore all of them into such tiny pieces that even if someone found them in the trash they'd have one hell of a time piecing them all back together. But who exactly would that somebody be? Who would care enough, my biographer, my lover? Grandiosity thy name was Len-ny then, and we were singing the same song. For good measure, the pension had an incinerator in back and I pushed all the scraps through its iron door. My guitar was next. I bashed it against the incinerator's rusted frame and shoved the pieces in. So there were witnesses to my madness. I wasn't just making it up to give myself an excuse. I was lucky they didn't kick me out right then. It's possible they didn't only because the old woman in black who had turned down my bed was the owner's mother or mother-in-law or something of that nature and had explained to her my grief.

I decided not to leave the island until I had seen Daphne's father. This could have been a problem because my plane ticket for Philadelphia was coming up soon and the start of law school which seemed at the moment like the most ridiculous thing in the world. Whose laws and for what? I mention this to someone who I know went to law school himself. Leonard, did you ever think to practice? Ha-ha, just a joke. Just distracting myself from what comes next. I had no idea when Daphne's father would return or if he would return. I could wait forever and it would serve me right. But there was no one else I could hope to talk to.

A week passed and one day the CLOSED sign on the shop turned to OPEN. In the meantime I had asked here and there about Daphne, about what was known, but mostly I kept to myself. I had not returned to the cliff. A good chance I was lying to myself then, but I thought I was nurturing myself back to sanity. Trying anyway. Len-ny, Len-ny. I heard that every night in my dreams. But what if I went up there and heard a rebuke? What if I went there and heard nothing at all? Best to put down markers, establish a perimeter. See things clearly, another joke intended for myself alone. In time I came to believe there was nothing up there but my dreams. That was my version of sanity. That and paying my respects to Daphne's father. The morning I walked into the shop he was at his adding machine. I loved that machine then. Small comfort, to press those hundred buttons, to choose which ones, to hear each one pushing down through its oiled slot, pressing against air itself, her father intent on doing it, the way my grandfather had done.

Hello Leonard, he said. Looking up from his calculations, accounts, whatever. Unlike Stavros from the hardware store, he was not into dramatic gestures. Maybe he had used them all up. He looked so tired. Infinitely tired I was going to write, but he didn't look to have the strength to do anything infinite. Infinite would have been too heavy a lift. It was like he was the definitive demonstration of someone the world had weighted down, gravity had picked him out to make an example of him, see here, you folks who think you can fly, take a long look, Einstein might be right in the big picture but here on Earth I'm still the boss.

Hello Mister Sarfatty, I said. Words weren't too kind to me then. They seemed to take a hike. I raised my arms in a kind of helplessness and shook my head.

I was a little distance from him. He had seen me enter and I had stopped when he saw me.

What do you want with us, he asked. I was struck by the us instead of, say, me, but no sooner was I struck with it, or possibly simultaneously, I became aware of a young boy in the back of the shop, by the door with the pebbled glass. I had expected it to be Annie, the omnipresent one, the shadow, but it was a boy with a somber, steady expression, not unfriendly, just uncertain. I felt an immediate affinity for his wariness.

Giannis, this is Mister Cohen, Sarfatty said in English, as though I were an opportunity for a lesson.

Yassas, hi, the boy said shyly, then he turned in seeming great fear and fled through the pebbled glass door.

Your son, I asked, and Sarfatty nodded, so there was that. Came down with the father after the funeral, I imagined. Daphne's little brother. I tried to remember if we had ever talked about Daphne having a brother. I couldn't remember.

His entering and leaving didn't do much for our conversation. What did I want with them? Finally I said I didn't want anything, but of course it wasn't quite true. If nothing else, information. With information if it's sturdy enough you can build walls, you can begin to wall things up. Somehow I feel this might have been in one of your songs, though I can't say which. Possibly all of them?

Daphne's father may have read my mind. He said all he knew was that she fell. He didn't curse me. He just kept his eyes down.

Finally I said the stupidest things about her, how brilliant she

78

was, her laugh, how lucky I was. I didn't say I loved her because I didn't want to be profane. I had seldom felt so strongly that if I told a lie I would be found out.

He didn't blame me, not in words anyway. And I'm not sure in any other way. I told him, because he was looking at it again, that my grandfather had had an adding machine like that and when I was a child I'd loved to play with it.

He asked me if I wanted to play with it now. I nodded and came behind the desk and pushed a few of the buttons and pulled the resistant lever that clicked when I pulled it and sprang back as it was supposed to. And the ringing sound, with each pull, as if something had been won. What Daphne was doing when I first saw her. Everything seemed familiar, everything seemed close, for a few seconds anyway. The old man had stepped back from the machine as I went to it. It's too old, I thought I heard him say. But still he didn't look at me much.

Somewhere in there as well I'm sure I added my little condolences, as though I'd been taught how to behave, my mama had brung me up right. And I'm sure he must have nodded. But I don't remember.

Before I left the island, I put together my theory of what had happened to Daphne. After the ferry left, after midnight, after she wandered around the town, she climbed the path to the cliff in order to watch the ferry make its way across the sea. She watched the receding lights and leaned forward to the cliff's edge so that she could see them a little longer, the only strings of pearls she would ever have, and she either tripped on a root and fell, or she leaned too far towards the fading lights and fell, or a gust of the meltemi got her and blew her off balance and she fell, or she jumped. After Daphne, the only stories I came to believe were the ones that could go one way or the other.

The fall itself, the tumble, the surprise, the flying, the fear or not, the panic or not, the feeling terribly sorry or not, the feeling terribly in love with life too late or not, I couldn't imagine. Not really. I didn't even want to try. Didn't want to go there, as they say. It seemed kind of obscene. Though possibly that was only my own fear talking.

Back in Athens I was surprised to find that Winston was still there. I ran into him in front of the American Express. He'd been with one of those girls with a k in her name and had missed his plane. He was waiting again for money from home. We hung out a little, caught up, I told him about Daphne but as little as possible. I didn't want his pity. But a funny thing. I didn't find it out then. Only years later, it was Beeler who told me. Winston really was CIA. Or let's put it this way, he was auditioning for the part. Earlier in the summer, before we all met up, he'd attended a student conference in Algiers as representative of some American student organization that was covertly CIA funded. Winston sent in a few notes, things he'd heard or seen. So there was that. In Vietnam he was assigned to army intelligence, so maybe the early CIA bit got him a little out of harm's way. Later of course he went to law school, like so many of the rest of us.

Would you, Leonard, have stayed or left? I'm pretty sure you would have left, just as Daphne said you would. And I don't know if you would have come back in a week. And would the leaving have been an act of cowardice or self-preservation?

Yours,

Leonard

22

Notes to any or all of the above, afterthoughts to disaster.

Daphne's high school education. But she read everything, she was a speed-reader, so there was a lot of catching up always going on. Her encyclopedia of opinions, too, who was this, who was that, the German Jews, a lot of others, as if the world would pay a price for keeping her out of school. It was no accident that she brought up Kierkegaard. The only accident would have been if she had been afraid to, afraid to frighten Leonard. If she would have used him for anything at all, it would not have been to get herself to America or for his sweet attentions or because she craved a body's warmth or because she mistook him for the "real" Leonard Cohen. But it might have been the temptation of anyone who has lived a life in books, to verify in the world what she had read.

The Temple of Apollo Metameleia, Apollo the Regretful. This was an outlier. Most shrines were devoted to the god's glorious aspects. Apollo Phoebus, the light of the sun. Apollo Lycegenes, born to a wolf. Apollo Acestor, the healer. Apollo Alexicacus, the protector. Apollo Manticus, the prophetic. Apollo Argyrotoxus, with the silver bow. Apollo Nymphegetes, the god of pastoral life. Apollo Archegetes, the founder.

The arrest of Michail Sarfatty. A year after Daphne's fall, her father was arrested in Thessaloniki and convicted of plotting subversion in connection with the printing of a leftist newspaper. He was sentenced to two years' exile under harsh conditions on a prison island. In his absence, his wife maintained the shop in Thessaloniki while Annie kept the store on S. running. But you could no longer buy *Das Kapital* or a Theodorakis record in either of them. After the colonels were overthrown, he ran for the Greek parliament from a working class district of Thessaloniki but lost, narrowly.

A thumbnail description of Leonard S. Cohen in 1968. He was five feet nine and weighed around one hundred forty with a thin face and a thin nose like a waterfall falling off a high mountain and lips that might have been thought to seek out others. He was dark-complexioned. Dark hair swept over his face and over his unappreciable ears. His intense eyes, set slightly far apart, asked sympathy without saying why. He parted his hair on the side.

Arguments in Leonard's mind for why she slipped. The rough terrain. The *meltemi* that was blowing strongly. Her possible loss of attention to exactly where she was on account of the receding ferry or what seemed its strings of pearls or some rehash of their last meeting or their last words together, whatever those were. The fact that he was coming back in a week, that he had promised. Or it was beside the point anyway, he could return or he could not, she didn't love him and there would be another and there had been others before him so why should she care, she had said it herself, summer romance. She was not the type to jump, though why she was not the type he couldn't say.

Arguments in Leonard's mind for why she jumped. She was familiar with the terrain so would have taken care unless she didn't care at all. She loved him more than she ever said or than he thought. Something about her past, about her mother or the suffering she saw as a child. Her disbelief that he was coming back in a week, and what difference would it make anyway, if he came and then he left again? He understood so little about her, all he could say for sure was that there were depths he hadn't a clue about and hadn't tried hard enough to fathom and there could have been anything in those depths, which still didn't mean she jumped but it did mean how could he ever know. That envelope with *drachma*s she was saving up for America.

Daphne and Leonard's mother. Yearning was what united them in Leonard's mind. Yearning and unfulfillment and vivid dreams, lights on distant marquees. Both of them provincials, both of them with a high school education. He didn't notice any of it at first. Only later. What some would call too late. Then, too, the Jewishness of it all, that he could only guess at. As though he'd been surrounded by something, like an atmosphere, like everything he'd ever breathed, and hadn't known it. Leonard's mother's name was Ellen. Later he troubled himself to discover Leonard N. Cohen's mother's name, Marsha.

Was it love? The question more interesting than the answer. Only ask the question. Keep asking the question. The best answer in the world might still fall off a cliff. And what about Hallmark? There's money to be made in them thar hills or off that selfsame cliff.

Photographs. Leonard took approximately half a roll on S. He had an old thirty-five millimeter camera that overexposed everything. Though perhaps that was the workman once more quarreling with his tools. The camera had no light meter and Leonard was bad at the settings and the brightness of the Aegean confounded him. When he got to Athens with two days to spare, he had the roll developed. There was Daphne leaning into the lens, her cheek darkening the frame, her dark hair in a spray, a rainbow glint off her sunglasses and the driving white light everywhere else. There was Daphne surprised in the shop, looking up from whatever she was doing in an embarrassment tipped with amusement, her blurred arm of protest only just beginning to be raised. There was Daphne on the esplanade, in the café, her sunglasses again, an iced coffee, a bit of shade, an easy smile. There was Daphne a moment later, looking put out, starting to look away, annoyed about what exactly, that he was wasting film? Or that she didn't like the way she looked and she had told him once already and still he was taking pictures? Only those four. How many more pictures would he have taken if he had known. Or none at all. On the rest of the roll were vapid shots of the sea or views from the bus to Panagia where the dirt of the windows streaked the sun or distant shots of the town like a long white ribbon signifying nothing.

The music in his life. He had been said to have a little bit of talent and was given a French horn, which he played until he was sixteen, at which point it occurred to him that sixteen-year-olds who played the French horn weren't, how to say it, pursuing a successful social strategy, so he dropped it and got a guitar. Though the guitar didn't solve the problem that he was shy. As to what he liked, he liked it all, and spent what he had on records, and it was only when he began to write his own songs that he began to narrow it down. Rock not so much. Acoustic over electric. Joni, Joanie, Dylan in descending order. Pete, too, and the Weavers, all the lefties strumming their hearts and minds. And then there was Leonard Cohen.

The legend of Apollo and Daphne, in a faded paperback edition Leonard would find at a library sale decades later. Insulted by some casual cutting remarks from the greater god, Eros shot one of his golden arrows at Apollo and a leaden one at the nymph Daphne. The god pursued her for conquest and she ran from him. About to be overtaken, desperate for escape at any price, she appealed for help to the river god her father, who cast a spell and, before Apollo's eyes, Daphne turned into a laurel tree. *Mollia cinguntur tenui praecordia libro, in frondem crines, in ramos bracchia crescunt.* There are versions other than Ovid's, perhaps as many as there were ever storytellers to tell them, but in all of them Apollo winds up grieving. Wearing his crown, playing his lyre, grieving. In the faded library-sale paperback, Leonard would find a plate of Bernini's marble Apollo and Daphne and realize that for sure the tree at the cliff's edge had been a laurel.

One conversation between Leonard and Daphne about the past:

Did you have relatives who died in the war, he said.

Of course, she said.

Many, he said.

I think so, of course, she said.

Your father's, your mother's, he said.

A brother came with my father to Istanbul, she said.

But the rest, he said.

The rest, yes, of course, she said.

Your mother got out too, he said.

We had family in Izmir who seemed to know the score before others did, she said.

Your parents met in Turkey, he said.

On a boat on the Bosporus, a little bit romantic even, she said.

Romantic and desperate, he said.

Everything was gone when they came back, she said.

But then you came along, he said.

In the other camp, in the DP camp, she said.

You must have been kind of a miracle, he said.

Of course, of course, she said.

The clothes Daphne wore. Those peasant blouses. Things she saw the tourists wear or buy, Cretan sacks, sandals, one skirt that was shorter than the others. But wild colors too. Scarves like she saw in magazines. She had a little bit the look of a sabra, or on worse days a woman of the Soviets, a new woman, halfway liberated. There was no sign she could sew, but her mother must have sewn, her scarcely mentioned mother.

23

Dear Leonard,

Dear Leonard, dear Leonard, dear Leonard. In those early days how I longed to have a friend. I've written you about my friends, about Winston, Harv, Beeler, but really we were more like buddies. If that's a distinction that makes any sense, I don't know. But it felt like it then. There were certain things we talked about, certain things we did together, certain memories we shared, but it felt strange and unrewarding to go further, a game with play money. In Athens I told Winston about Daphne. Not about the tree but about the rest of it. And his reaction seemed well-meaning enough, and comforting, he even wanted to take me out and get me drunk. But I didn't want to get drunk. And he was fine with that too. Finally I realized it was my fault. I was withholding part of the story. The tree, the voice, the craziness. It was my insincerity, or my sense of the limits that our friendship could bear. I longed for somebody I could spill my guts to. And it occurred to me, just from the record I'd heard, that that friend could be you. You were my rival, my goad, you were everything before Daphne's death that disturbed my mind, yet I longed for you to be my friend.

An overactive imagination? A grasping at straws? I was young. Maybe that's all it was. Being young. Being young and losing something.

And again on the question of whether she slipped or she

jumped. I told myself to be objective. I steeled myself for either possibility. Yet I was almost glad I couldn't know for sure. All the legends I'd ever heard where you're punished for wanting to know too much. Going all the way back. The Genesis of Leonard S. Cohen and where would it all come out? Better to accept the stalemate. I was where I was. I longed to know, but only from the comfort of my own mind. I became again almost convinced that the voice coming from the tree was nothing more than the wind.

So would you have been my friend back then? Probably not. Though I might have been an acolyte. Say, if you had still been on Hydra when I was there, or had already come back, a star on the rise, and I met you in a café. I was younger, I was nobody, I had a few songs. A dime-a-dozen type of Leonard Cohen. Not the real article.

Sure, why not, an acolyte maybe. A crowd, a bunch of people in the café, Americans, Canadians, you and I. Oh, you're Leonard Cohen? I'm Leonard Cohen too. And so what? What to make of it? A secret acolyte. Instead of to me you pay your attention to the pretty girls at the table, or to your friends. Or maybe Marianne is there. Beeler and Harv and Winston and I, if that's the configuration, or two of us, or three of us, whichever number, we seem, actually, a little bit like everything you've escaped. Yet, if I hung on, if I persisted, an acolyte, maybe? Probably not a friend. Not then.

I could have gone back to Hydra instead of flying to Philadelphia. But I flew to Philadelphia. Now I can point to the most obvious reason of all, the draft. You Canadians had it so easy. No colonial war to fight, no saving the world from the commie menace, no misguided best-and-brightests telling all of you what to do, maybe getting you killed. But, still, I could have stayed, and fuck the draft, come get me if you will.

But I didn't. I flew to Philadelphia with my grief in my luggage.

Yours,

Leonard

24

Everyone has a moment when the rest of their life begins. Leonard entered law school, telling himself it was just another bourgeois folk tale coming true, asking himself what the hell was he doing. But he was there. The whole country was coming apart that year yet the law schools were full. Who were all these people? People going about the business of their lives. And so was he, a weekend warrior at best. It turned out the draft wasn't taking the likes of him that selfsame year, one leg shorter than the other or whatever it was, hundreds of reasons, hundreds of excuses, filling inboxes like sad little notes to the teacher, and the law schools stayed full. Hadn't Ali given all who wanted it the ur-excuse of them all: *I ain't got no quarrel with them Vietcong*. Though there were moments, too, when Leonard imagined he should go to Vietnam as a penance for Daphne. Even if she hated that war, and called it a colonial war, and it was from her that he picked up the phrase. She would not have wanted him to go. She would have hidden him on a Greek island. She said that too.

He buried himself in torts and contracts so that he could be alone with his own mind. Who did what to whom, who agreed to what with whom. Who, whom, he hated it, hated all the whoms. It was still the year of revolution. And yet. Daphne began to recede, just a little, in his mind. There wasn't time. If he gave up the law, he would start writing songs again. If he gave up the law, he would think all the time about Daphne. It was a kind of cure, an ice bath of reason, making all the arguments in the world and not caring about any of them. A year passed and he survived it.

And in the second year of it came the thought that it was something he could do, make those arguments. He was even not too bad at it, when he forced his mind to it, when he pried it away from Daphne and the Leonard Cohen who was out there and the songs he would never write and the ambition that was from before the rest of his life that had now begun. How banal, how ordinary, the predictability of nothing more startling than what goes up must come down. Yet he was getting used to it. He lived in a room smaller than he had ever lived in. He often remembered how he'd imagined Daphne being with him there, the problems, the kitchen-sink melodrama. Was it a proof now of all he had feared or was he only making one more excuse to lengthen his list of fools?

He lived his life, the old day-at-a-time trick or that's what it seemed. He imagined working for a nonprofit. He imagined getting a government job. Or living humbly, moving to Vermont, the country, a whole earth catalog life, that too. And he began, just a little, to listen to music again. The music of that year, a good year for music. Why couldn't he just listen, why did he have to compete? He was out of that now. He had lost. And so what? A thousand runners start the marathon and one guy wins. But the other nine hundred ninety-nine guys, what happens to them? Do they just find a ditch and lie down and die? There were drugs around, too, and Leonard tried them, a little anyway, the way a law student would try them, on the weekends or to calm down. He was becoming a consumer of the culture. No more a maker of it, not that he ever had been. But it was more that he knew his place now. And on one of the weekends as a consumer of the culture he dropped mescaline.

It came with a bullshit myth from a shaggy guy next to him in his Trusts section about how it had come from a secret special place in Mexico, a place with a shaman atop every cactus so to speak, and the shaggy guy was going with some others to see an eclipse on the Jersey Shore and the mescaline was for that and Leonard went along, though he never made it to the eclipse. Along the way in the back of the bus the cosmic joke of the drug got to him and he began seeing Daphne behind every bush or really they weren't bushes but rather trees, and he'd never in his life wanted to have sex so much as then but it wasn't to be. How long might this be going on, he wondered, and regretted he hadn't asked the question before, and if the bus was going to go on forever he would not approve. Help me, Daphne, help me, Daphne, he must have said aloud before she disappeared and he grew very afraid on account of all the falling going on, his falling or the world falling, or the forever aspects of it all, so that the only other thing he said aloud on the whole trip was "I want to die." The others, whoever they were, heard it and didn't wish to be responsible, especially the shaggy guy who had a future in the law to think about, so they took him to an emergency room where a nurse injected him and he slept it off. Later he felt he perhaps hadn't said "I want to die," but rather something more like "I don't want to die alone." In either case he went home and studied for Trusts on Sunday. The others, on account of the detour, missed getting to the Jersey Shore, which was declared by all a bummer, the old catch basin of every misfortune, but they saw half an eclipse anyway from the side of the road. Every-one wore dark glasses as they should. Leonard later felt it was all the same, or almost the same, the mescaline and when he heard Daphne's voice coming from the tree on S. The only dif-ference, he felt, was that one was real and the other wasn't, but he wasn't sure which one was which. So there was that. End of another story, in a way.

In his final year of law school it seemed that Leonard had matured. Or it might have seemed so to a certain type of observer, for whom maturity was a natural consequence of life, but Leonard himself was less sure. All he knew really was that he had taken loans that he would soon have to start paying back. The usual suspects revisited his mind, a public defender's office, a poverty clinic, a country lawyer's office, but one day on a bulletin board he saw that a small law firm in Beverly Hills, California was coming to interview candidates. He felt a repugnance that went with the territory about Beverly Hills, the antithesis in 1970 of every counterculture dream, but something in the firm's self-description caught his attention. Among its clients were singers and artists and others in the music field. No names were mentioned, and Leonard understood this to be proper. But he was enough intrigued to sign up. He had never been to California. He had only the vaguest idea even where the continental divide was or, for that matter, what it was.

The interviewing partner was surprisingly without Hollywood flash. Leonard imagined they sent him east with exactly that unassumingness in mind. He did talk about a boom in the business of entertainment, and the weather, and the Dodgers, and for some reason the new art museum, as if, my God, look, we've got culture, too. It was all like a little tour. Leonard felt that he was even being courted. And maybe he was. The best and the brightest didn't want those jobs in those years. The interviewer for most of the interview ignored the obvious but, at the very end, as if it were a little joke to cap the afternoon, he said we don't represent Leonard Cohen. Leonard smiled weakly.

But secretly he thought how remarkable it would have been if they did. What a sign, what a coincidence, what a blessing. But even if they didn't, even if they only came close enough to make a joke about it. Maybe they would someday, or maybe they wouldn't. Or maybe, as intimated, they already represented others in the so-called music firmament. How much fun would that be? A little anyway. Keeping his hand in, that sort of thing. If he couldn't do it himself, at least helping those who could. It would be an act of humility, too, a recognition of what was what in the world. The firm, Babbington and Kravitz, offered him the job. When the guy called up to make the offer, he again saved the punchline for last. "Hey, we're not going to be a firm representing music people and pass up having a Leonard Cohen on board."

And quite likely, Leonard thought, it was true. He got the job on account of his name.

But getting a respectable job in a field akin to a long-time obsession wasn't the end of the evolution of Leonard Cohen during his last year in law school. He met Carolyn Ritter. She was in his class and going his way, being from Pasadena and having landed a job in a downtown L.A. firm where a darkened portrait of a great-grandfather loomed in the lobby. Car, as everyone called her in a class that had exactly fourteen women, was not the first girl he'd dated in Philadelphia. Even law students took time off to get laid if they could, and a few times Leonard took his chances. It was still the sixties after all, the sixties turning seventy. The others were as dismissible to him as Leonard was to them, names not forgotten but only a little remembered, a list in everybody's drawer. But with Car, something stuck. There was no meet-cute. In fact, neither could quite point to the moment when they became aware of the other's existence. In Real Property?

Commercial Transactions? The cafeteria between the Jell-O and the pudding? It became a running joke with them, and for awhile they lived off running jokes. Leonard made the point which in his view she would have to accept as valid that since there were only fourteen women in the class, it would be only logical and inevitable that he spotted her first. She argued that she had always liked his glasses. He had gotten new glasses the year before and they made him look a little like a Beatle. In any event they managed to stay apart from one another for two and a half years and then met in a snowstorm when she was shoveling her car out and he offered to help. She would rather have declined, for feminist-political reasons, but a blister had developed between her thumb and her forefinger from the shovel so she said yes. She had a VW, which was not a heavy car, and Leonard eventually pushed it out. Talks, coffees, walks, bed. He loved her look, which was extremely blonde, almost white, as though on a ski slope she would be nearly invisible. White eyebrows, white hair, glacial eyes. And she really did like his glasses. His glasses, her body, and they were both fairly ironic, about their situation, about themselves. And they argued the way law students argued, almost for the fun of it, lion cubs of the mind. Daphne dropped out of his dreams, the ones anyway that he could remember.

25

Dear Leonard,

There's a lot I could say about Car. But to begin with the obvious: I was attracted to her. Sexually, to her look, to her body, all that part of it. I know, I know, superficial, won't last, all the tut-tutters having their say. But, actually, to me, that very sexual attraction was why I thought it would last. It wasn't going away, I knew that much. Not that I thought very much, in the early days, about whether or not it would last. I was happy simply to see her every day, to argue with her, to kid around with her. It was so convenient, too, I suppose. Same school, same year, some of the same classes, headed in the same geographic direction. Most nights she came to my tiny room or I went to hers. One thing very specific: she loved Hemingway, kind of her favorite writer, she loved even the macho stuff. So of course I brushed up on my Hemingway. Which is a blatant exaggeration, as I'd never read much of him before to brush up on, but I read a little anyway. "A great talent and appreciation for the bed." Somewhere in there I read that line about somebody. And that was Car, or close to it. A talent for the bed. It's what I thought then. And there wasn't any-thing dirty about it either, and it wasn't fantasyland. She simply had it. She was unashamed. And a little bit athletic, too, as if she might have fitted nicely in a nudist community. There are those, I'm sure, who might find that boring after awhile, but I didn't. Maybe it was only that I still knew too little about the world. I had this dream of becoming as healthy as she was, or she providing enough of it for us both. She was lithe. Is that an unfair word?

It didn't hurt to have the whole Jew/Gentile thing going on. But Car was also more than the Scandinavian girls we idiots once chased around, or anyway more than what we saw in them. She was my intellectual equal. Actually, she was better at the law school thing than I was, or it's possible she simply cared more. She saw the world with a certain clarity, yes or no, this or that. When she spoke, it was in whole sentences. No shortcuts for her. And have I mentioned her eyes? Later she became a litigator. I always feared for the witness who had to face those eyes.

But to go back. We did joke around a lot. Both of us thought we were going through a kind of purgatory but that our terms would soon be up. California beckoned. She could get fairly obnoxious talking about it, so then I would brag about upstate New York, its welcoming snow, its ample dairy production. And would we live together out there? Car talked about her parents then, who might or might not approve, and here the Jew/Gentile thing invariably returned, whether we mentioned it out loud or not. They were some sort of Pasadena royalty, I was given to believe. Her father a retired rear admiral and lawyers and bankers and ranchers everywhere else and friends of people I'd never heard of, Huntingtons for one. Who did I have to offer, two generations of Cohens and their hardware store? Uncle Mo Cohen the bookie of Joseph Avenue? Again I played the irony card as best I could. But it would be a lie to say I wasn't impressed by Car's lineage, and that's even with not having thought about it much before. Though maybe that's something she found attractive: my relative ignorance, my short memory in that department. I'm not even going to go into the first time I met the esteemed Ritters. Or, actually, I guess I am. It had all the chances of being a movie scene, with my parents coming down for graduation and Car's flying in

98

from Pasadena, a culture clash full of awkwardness and gaffes, possibly a little vulgarity thrown in for laughs, but my mother thankfully caught a flu a few days before and the esteemed Cohens of upstate had to cancel. So that left me going out to dinner with the Admiral and Sally Ritter. Who were perfectly nice, of course. Going <u>way</u> out of their way. I can't think of a single embarrassing question they asked. Republicans, of course. He golfed. She gardened. This was before I knew that everyone in Pasadena originally came from Ohio or Indiana.

Car loved to sail. I didn't know how to sail. Car rode. I didn't. Car loved to work up a sweat. I could take it or leave it. Car had ceased to believe in God. I had never quite started, thus didn't have the same antipathy. So we had our differences. I could make a longer list. We, let's just say, found the differences invigorating. We drove out to Los Angeles in her Beetle arguing most of the way and screwing in every motel and somewhere halfway between her job downtown and mine in Beverly Hills we found a one-bedroom apartment and began to settle down.

Work became us. Is that the right way to say it? I don't mean we became our work, I mean it seemed to make us better with each other. It was almost like a continuation of school. The long hours, the long paragraphs of fine print demanding not to be ignored, keeping our minds busy enough, leaving some of the arguing in the office. Car probably always liked it more than I did. Her downtown firm, which was fairly huge, represented an oil company but tried to balance the books with pro bono work. Or at least it was something to put in their annual report, and to ease the consciences of junior associates like Car. Babbington and Kravitz likewise let us go get an occasional burglar out of jail but mostly it was the tedious messes and ambitions of film and TV production companies that we were hired to sort out, satisfy, or make go away, which was both more and less fun than that

99

description might make it seem. We of course had our music busi-
ness clients too. I won't mention names. The most surprising part
to me was that I actually got paid quite well for doing this. Not
so much, maybe, as the guys who went to Wall Street, but it didn't
seem quite as soul-destroying either. There was that rub, however
distant, with people who for better or worse were remaking the
culture every day. That's how I looked at it, "for better or worse,"
because of course I saw a lot of the worse. Then Car got pregnant
and we got married on the fly and bought a little house in West-
wood and all of that began.

I'm not going to belabor my career in child-rearing. A family
man. Never quite imagined it, then there it was. And I liked it,
loved the kids beyond reason, did the dad thing. Little Dave, fol-
lowed with almost undue haste by little Mark. Both of us, Car
and I, became unspeakably, predictably boring on the subject of
our kids, on subjects related to child-rearing more generally. I
will say that I tried to resist this, but I can't say that Car did.
She worked half-time for awhile. We moved to a bigger house in
Cheviot Hills. The kids grew up to be bruisers. Stars in school,
baseball, track. Her genes, not mine. Though maybe I always had
the hand-eye thing. Am I getting ahead of myself, going too fast? It
always seemed like it went very fast. Worth mentioning, though, I
suppose, are the epic fights we had over how to raise the kids. She
was more authoritarian, I was more live-and-let-live or maybe
teach-by-example. That one we never sorted out. I suppose the
kids got a little of each and it didn't seem to do them much harm.
There was one partner at Babbington I particularly liked, an old
Armenian guy, kind of emeritus at the firm, who as they say had
seen it all, like he was a kid in Turkey when the Turks tried to
kill all the Armenians. And he said to me, even before Dave was
born, that for some people it could maybe be different but for the
average guy like himself, which by extension I knew he meant me,

the only thing in life that lasted was family. I took that to heart. I had no means, finally, to resist it.

Though while we're on the subject of family, an interesting development, about fifteen years in. Old Rear Admiral Ritter, that exemplar of WASP probity, got indicted for insider trading. It turned out he had received a tip from his brother the equally exemplary investment banker and shorted IBM the morning before a terrible earnings report. The brother was indicted as well. This was of course a calamity for Car, and it didn't exactly enhance our family's sense of self-worth, but I couldn't help but feel a bit of secret satisfaction. Mo Cohen may have been a bookie but he was never indicted, that kind of thing. And as it happened, it was I, Leonard, more than Car, who was able to do a little something to help the old admiral out. At Babbington there was a guy doing securities who'd recently been an assistant U.S. attorney in the Central California office and he put in a few words with the guy there who had the case. Who knows if it did any good, but the admiral got sixty days instead of what could have been two and a half years. And what thanks did I get? No good deed goes unpunished, right? The admiral was short of money on account of all his legal bills. We had to start bailing him out.

If you were to google "Leonard Cohen lawyer Los Angeles area," instead of just plain Leonard Cohen—I found this out in later years—what you could find is reference to the Goldstein Bakery case. Now I'm not going to go into all the details, but it was a pioneering case in its field, in some ways. It was in any event my most significant achievement. It made some law in the field of implied contracts in cases of employee disability. I was a little proud of it at the time. I also had a hand in one of the earliest palimony cases in California. It might have been like the fifteenth case. I am aware of the irony in these descriptions. I am aware it doesn't sound like much. But to me it meant a little something. I made partner at Babbington after seven years. And that was despite never being much of a rainmaker. You know what a rainmaker is, a guy who brings in work? I seldom brought in work. I didn't play golf. I detested golf. But I was diligent and a little inventive when it came to the case work, and it turned out not everybody was. As well, I seemed to have the ability to write nice clear briefs, which once in a while someone would even call elegant. In the meantime the kids grew up. Dave went off to Middlebury. Mark went off to Bucknell. Neither of them wanted their dad's old alma mater and it turned out his old alma mater didn't want them. All those hundred-dollar checks wasted. Car made partner, too, a couple of years after I did. The classic child-rearing delay, but she made it. And I would say we were all really proud of her. We moved to a bigger house in the Palisades, a house with an ocean view. I expanded my CD collection. This was my hobby, you could probably say. We're talking about before streaming, before the iTunes store, before all of it, and I wound up with approximately four thousand CDs. Car found it really obnoxious or obsessive. Once she suggested I should see a shrink about it. But I had slowly come to love music again. All kinds of music. I had a library where I would go in every night, or anyway most nights—a few nights I wouldn't so as not to piss off Car too much—and listen. A bit of an audiophile, too. Spent chunks on equipment. And why not? I was a consumer of the culture after all. I was finally that. I was a bourgeois and proud of it. Or at least not too embarrassed by it. How could I be? It was what I had done and become. Car, by way of offset, bought a little sailboat and joined the yacht club in Marina del Rey. Or maybe it wasn't an offset at all, maybe it was just her joy. The admiral's daughter, after all. The disgraced admiral, maybe, but does a daughter care? I actually loved her for that. I loved to see her sail her little boat as I'd once loved to see her just walking around, so in command, so

*confident, so—that silly word again—lithe. Both the boys, mean-
while, graduated and stayed in the east. Mark had a little hippie
in him and went to Vermont, started work on an organic farm.
Dave dropped out of business school after three months, went to
New York, got a job with a start-up. This was sufficiently before
the first dot-com bust. So things were moving right along. Youth,
middle age, coming up soon enough late middle age. Then one
day Car came in after work and over the chicken pot pie dinner
said she was filing for divorce.*

Yours,

Leonard

26

One of the partners at Car's downtown firm had a bigger boat than she had and one day they went sailing on the bigger boat and one thing led to another. It must have been a pretty nice boat because Car had had an affair or two before and it had never led to a petition for divorce; this being Leonard's dark voice talking to himself, taken by surprise, trying to get a hold, still the seeker of solace in the ironies life in its half-sleep dreams up, still willing himself to feel better about it all. At least she'd had the good taste to wait until the kids were out of the house. She had always had good taste, Leonard thought, more good taste than good sense. Though he could see the good sense to it too. Why shouldn't she leave? They had had their run. Raised the kids right, more or less. Bought the house with the ocean view. Those vows of till-death-do-us-part, had he even paid much attention when they were standing in the courthouse? The stuff for the late night comedians, those vows, these days.

And so nothing if not fair-minded was this not-yet-quite-late-middle-aged lawyer to the mostly not-quite stars.

Yet he tried bitterly to keep her. He missed her, in the morning across the bed and at other times. Or really all the time for awhile, as time itself slowed down, which was all as it was supposed to be, he could remember even from grade school crushes, and this had been twenty-six years. Still, he demanded therapists, he demanded couples counseling, the whole rigmarole destined to go nowhere, a snake eating its tail. The guy with the bigger boat was getting a divorce himself. He lived in Pasadena, so what did you expect? Don't even mention his name, but he was tall the way Leonard was not. He had some money, too, as Leonard came to understand it with a little carefully concealed help from a private security agency, so with his half and her half the couple of sailors would be doing fine. Sully and Car, there, he said it. Sounds good enough, it would work on the Christmas card. As for the affairs before Sully that Leonard imagined she had had, she hadn't. Not in reality, though she may have dreamed. Leonard wrote her, Leonard rallied the boys to help, Leonard offered to buy her an America's Cup yacht ha-ha or an emoji or two, then he gave up, slowly, but he did. She didn't want the house in the Palisades so he stayed there. He didn't want it either, but neither could he bear the thought of cleaning it out and seeing it empty, the holes in the wall where the pictures had hung, the dust behind the refrigerator.

Occasionally he would still review the conversation over the chicken pot pie, her saying I want a divorce, him holding his fork midair and saying what did you say, her saying you heard me, him saying of course I heard you but do you really mean that, her saying haven't you noticed I've been unhappy, him saying actually what I've noticed is you've been happier, her saying yes, there's someone. Shortened a little, for the clarity of oozing, spreading memory, but there it was, over and over, and even with her getting a little emotional so that Leonard thought this must be hard for her, and she's upset but doesn't really mean it, the conversation always came out the same. So if it wasn't going to change, Leonard would have to change. A therapist told him that, but just because a therapist told him didn't necessarily mean it was a lie. Leonard began to shut the old conversation off. Don't darken my door, that sort of thing. Regrets, chicken croquettes. The boys are doing fine, don't worry about the boys. It was the start of the era of internet dating, and Leonard looked at himself and thought, am I consumer of the culture or am I not? Do I have a decent income? Do I still have hair? Middle-aged man's rim shot but what the hell. He realized, too, that he'd likely had fewer sex partners in life than the typical American male. A study of British men online claimed an average of sixteen point one partners for the cousins, so could Americans be far behind?

Leonard felt he should at least catch up and be average or if at all possible slightly above, and so he set to work. He had the time, after all, and the inclination, and the house with an ocean view, an American trifecta of sorts. And of course it was fun for awhile, a diversion at the least, until he got to number thirteen on the playlist. Nothing against thirteen, a pleasant and talkative woman in her forties who had relocated from Wichita to work as a secretary at Disney, a starting-over story like his own, but as they did the dance on their second date he found he was counting time in his head to the rhythm of the strokes, and what kind of fun was that, to be the John Philip Sousa of sex?

He would have thrown the whole project over, there would have been no number fourteen at all, but then he met Amelia, Mella for short, and it wasn't even on Jdate or one of those, it was in the elevator of the building Babbington had moved to in Century City. They were the only two going up and a five-dollar bill fell out of her unzipped bag getting off. The old-fashioned way. Five floors separated them. Lunch downstairs in the sterile skyscraper courtyard, a walk on the weekend, a few galleries. Genteel enough, slow enough. She was a few years younger but not many, she had nice cheekbones and a dimpled chin, there was a trimness to everything about her as if she had learned not to throw herself too much into the world, possibly a line of defense but drawn cleanly and without malice. A convert to Judaism, too. Having grown up West Texas Baptist, having run off, having married one Elliot Gotbaum who had the poor manners to leave her by way of a fatal coronary at age forty-seven, having never had a child on account of plumbing issues that no fertility clinic could repair. She seemed to like Leonard quite a bit. She worked for an insurance company that insured pets. She was a quiet person, which Leonard liked. They even walked on the beach a little, which made Leonard feel like he was in an ad for life insurance. He told her that. Her sense of humor wasn't great, or maybe his jokes weren't great, he was willing to entertain either possibility or maybe both were true. Then came the stumbling block of her Judaism. She belonged to a synagogue in the Valley. Most Saturday mornings she went. After a couple of months they were talking about Mella moving in, and not for the first time she offered that if he felt like it he should come with her to the synagogue, her tact in offering being part and parcel of his reluctance every other time she'd asked. You don't really believe I'm a Jew, she said. You don't really believe *I'm* a Jew, he said. The stalemate persisted. As if to tempt him, Mella spoke quite often of her rabbi, a wonder-worker named Menachem Steinman with a great golden beard and a voice like honey who, after Elliot died, she said, was a great solace and comfort to her. Leonard mostly nodded like a judicious sage, taking the tales of wonder in, but finally he looked up Menachem Steinman on the internet. The photo of him showed the great beard, so golden it looked to Leonard fake, like the henna beards he had sometimes seen of Afghan elders. But behind the golden beard Leonard followed Steinman's trail, from Brooklyn to Jerusalem to the West Bank settlements to a rabbi also once from Brooklyn who believed that Eretz Israel the promised land was one and whole from the Nile to the Euphrates, meaning no room for the Arabs in between. And what to do with them? The Arabs were not Rabbi Schatzow's problem. Moreover, wrote Rabbi Schatzow, the Sixth Commandment didn't apply to Gentiles. Leonard told Mella that she belonged to a nationalistic cult, an evil right-wing plot. Mella said how could there be a nationalistic right-wing plot in the San Fernando Valley? Leonard said he didn't know but there it was. She pleaded with him to come see for himself, until finally he did. On a Saturday morning they drove from the Palisades to Ventura Boulevard, a decidedly down-market journey. Rabbi Steinman's congregation met in a storefront that had formerly been an appliance store, low-ceilinged and nearly windowless, with folding chairs and a makeshift bimah. Rabbi Steinman was as advertised, his golden beard, his honey voice, a robust man of forty, and the dancing and singing were as advertised, and the joy of the Torah brought from hand to hand through the throng. Before it was over there was a fundraising pitch that went on longer than Rabbi Steinman's sermon for an organization called Branch of Life, doing lifesaving work in Eretz Israel. Later Leonard looked up Branch of Life. It had been founded by Rabbi Jacob Schatzow in the occupied lands. You can't have a Sixth Commandment and it only applies to not killing Jews, Leonard said to Mella. Rabbi Steinman never said that, Mella said. His teacher said it, Leonard said. You're an antisemite, Mella said. Sticks and stones, Leonard said. I apologize, she said. Apologize for what, he said. For calling you that, she said. But Mella never moved in and soon he began to see her less.

Leonard had more time for listening. It may have been in the liner notes for a Ravi Shankar album that he first heard of a certain Indian way of life, perhaps even no longer practiced, or anyway practiced less, where a family man, once his family is grown and his wife is cared for and his householding duties are complete, will leave the village or wherever he has lived and go into the forest to seek a holy man or his soul. Leonard felt he might just have reached that time of life, but where was the forest and where was the holy man?

27

Dear Leonard,

Over the years, as you can imagine, there was a certain amount of continuing witty repartee that I was subject to, about our names, the result of being on the periphery of the music business. People surprised that I had given up my fabulous musical career out of devotion to that jealous mistress the Law, and on like that, years of variation on a theme. But at the same time, you might be more surprised to know, I had developed a bit of a reputation on my own. Leonard Cohen, over at Babbington, the lawyer Leonard Cohen, to distinguish from the musical one, good guy to wrap up deals, attentive to the details, a bulldog when he has to be. And of course I got used to all that.

But there was something about losing Car, and to a much lesser yet measurable degree Mella, which put me back toward confusing you with me. Maybe it was nothing more than the time on my hands. If I'd been younger, I might have plunged myself into work. But I felt too old to do that. I couldn't fool myself that way. Does that make as much sense as it should? I imagine you might have felt the same at times. It takes stronger and stronger medicine the older you get. Old drunks, too. But I'd never been much of a drinker.

Instead there were all my records. Excuse me, CDs. Excuse me, MP3s. I suppose I shouldn't complain. All those people buying one thing then the same thing over in a different format, were great for a lawyer who had clients like mine. Maybe the companies were losing money as things got cheaper and cheaper, maybe the artists, but not the lawyers. Anyway, my point is, as I listened to my music every evening, I listened more and more to you. It was kind of inevitable, really. You were always my favorite. I'd forgotten how I somehow blamed you for Daphne, as I'd almost forgotten Daphne. And what an odd thing, anyway, as though shifting the blame onto a magical figure. It was I who left, not you. Would you have done the same, would you have not done the same. I was inspired, that's all. I left because I wanted to. It's possible I found out all these things in your songs.

And there was another factor as well, concerning you, concerning me. I had read somewhere, probably in the LA Weekly, that you were living on Mount Baldy, had entered the monastery there. You know, I almost imagined I could see your monastery from my office. Babbington was on a high floor. My office faced east. On a clear day the San Gabriels loomed. It took me awhile to figure out which one was Baldy but, once I did, I might look out on those clear days and think, I can see where he lives. And I wondered what you were doing in that monastery, so I bought books on Zen Buddhism. Now I am aware that you can't get the essence of Zen Buddhism from a book. The books tell you that, so there's no chance of making that mistake more than once. But what I did get from my reading might surprise you. It certainly surprised me. I began thinking again about Daphne. The noth-ingness, the void, the yearning to escape suffering, the steps you might take or not take, all things for which the words I know are inadequate, as I even knew then they were inadequate, yet they made me think of her. I'm not sure I can even say why. More than that, I don't want to say why.

Only this. What I began to think, or really to feel, as I read those books or listened to your latest or looked out from my office

window on a clear day at Mount Baldy, was that what I expe-
rienced during those short weeks I spent with Daphne was an
intimacy greater than any I had ever felt since.

   Yours,

   Leonard

28

Dear Leonard,

One thing I might add, since I've mentioned it before and I'm sure you'll know what I'm talking about. It was an intimacy akin to what I felt on mescaline, yes, but that had been an intimacy only with myself. How do you measure intimacy? Do you call it greater or lesser, nearer or farther, more real or less? Daphne had been so alive.

Yours,

Leonard

29

Dear Leonard,

And the tree. And the voice.

Yours,

Leonard

30

It would be an adventure the end of which he could not predict. On a weekend morning in February 1999, after a winter storm had passed through, Leonard searched online and made calls to determine if chains would be required for a drive into the San Gabriel mountains. In Los Angeles after a winter storm, the snow-capped mountains loom over the city. The city itself may be sunny and seventy degrees, bringing fatuous smiles back to the faces of the TV weathermen, but the mountains in their bride-like sudden whiteness beckon and instruct. Or was "adventure" the wrong way to put it? "Pilgrimage" might have been closer to what he was feeling. As if after decades he would join forces with what had always been out there. He had read all the books. He had no idea what he would say.

It was like following a kind of geometry for Leonard to seek out the Mount Baldy Zen Center. The Highway Patrol informed him that chains would be required. He made further calls to find out where chains could be had. He drove east on the freeways with his heart in a bubble and stopped at a Denny's for pancakes and then in Claremont for the chains. There was no rhyme or reason to it, only that he was doing it at last. Or closer to the truth: the longer he drove, the closer he got, the more he disavowed his reasons, or ceased to believe them. But he continued to drive. After Claremont there was suburban sprawl, then a turnoff and the road was narrower and began to climb. The chains clanked and he slowed down. There were switchbacks and, soon after four thousand feet, snow tipped the still-brown land. Then after that the snow was deep, piled to the roadside by one pass of a plow, and everywhere in the trees and crowning the boulders. How fitting, Leonard thought. Perhaps it was what he had been waiting for all along, the snow, still deep and clean, so that the boy from upstate New York and the boy from across the lake and up the river could finally meet. Leonard wondered if Leonard had loved the snow as he had, waking up mornings to deliver the papers in it, the neighbors' porches piled high with it, the rails, the steps, fluffy and untouched, like clouds that had landed on Earth. But then he remembered that the other Leonard, the rich kid Leonard, would not have gotten up mornings to deliver papers. A pity, Leonard thought. But he might still have loved the snow. Maybe he'd talk to him about it, about Montreal, about Rochester, about snow.

There was a dip in the road then an unmarked gravel drive, which was what his directions said there would be, so he turned down the drive and slowed further down. All around him were scatters of dusted pines and ahead in the middle of the pines a few places for cars to park and the simple brown buildings of the monastery. There were a few signs pointing here or there but nothing that told him where to go. No one was about. He got out of his car and walked across the lightly shoveled ground. There were several doors that to Leonard looked all the same. He was chilled and he liked that part of it. He wore the parka and gloves that were like new and that Car had insisted he would need for the weekends when with a happy face she took them all to ski. Another point of contention. Who cared about any of that now, but it's funny it's what he thought of. He mounted a few steps where it looked like the snow had been stepped on and knocked on a plain door. No one answered and he knocked again, lightly so as not to be a pest, and when no one answered he went to the next building down and knocked on the door there. Everywhere there was silence, only the whistling in the pines. He knocked on a few more doors. *Gornisht*, as his old-school relatives used to say. He went back to his car and waited and looked around. After half an hour he turned the engine on to keep warm. They must all be meditating, he thought. He wondered if it was a special occasion. The largest of the buildings was dark. It had windows but what he would not do was go peek in. What kind of insult would that be? What if there really were people inside, looking back at his strange peering face? He imagined their ruined meditations coming crashing down on him. Then a monk—what else would Leonard call him if not a monk—came out of one of the doors in a black robe. He was tall, dark, and Western-looking but he was not Leonard Cohen. He was too young, perhaps too tall. Leonard got out of the car and walked after him. Excuse me, excuse me, I'm a visitor, Leonard said, could you tell me is there an office or someone I could speak to? The monk turned to him and he was not Leonard Cohen for sure and made a gesture like zip-the-lip, his finger zipping across his mouth, though his mouth when he did it looked friendly enough, like a DO NOT DISTURB sign but lightly drawn.

So Leonard had interrupted a silent retreat. It was all a guess. Everything was a guess. This bothered Leonard. He felt like a fool, then an interloper, then a burglar, stealing something he could not even name. He waited another hour in the car, just to be sure, keeping his eyes peeled, looking around at the snow, the clouds on Earth. No one else appeared, then he left.

31

Dear Leonard,

I tried to find you once, on Mount Baldy, then I let it go. It was as though the silence of the one monk I found there enveloped me as well. I can remember the rattling of the chains on my car, thinking they were making a fool of me, as I drove down from the mountain. Did you love the snow, Leonard, when you were young? I had hoped to ask you that.

Fast forward. Isn't that what people used to say? Or maybe they still do, even if the buttons where it used to be written are mostly dreams now. Anyway, fast forward a few years. And my life entered, shall we say, its uninteresting phase. Though I'm not even sure what I mean by that. I suppose not that I lost interest in it, but that I became more aware of the possibility that others had little interest in it. The feeling of going shopping in a store and nobody really noticing that you were there. The feeling of being the sort of person that you yourself didn't use to notice. The days seemed to go slow in person and fly by in retrospect. Or maybe it was only that there were so many more days to remember and they all piled up together. I began to understand with a bitter nostalgia that old silly movie shot where they would show the pages of the calendar ripping off and flying away.

But, I guess you'd say equally, I found that "getting on" had its compensations. Nothing exceptional, just the garden-variety compensations. There was no one around to tell me what to do or think badly of me. I could admire my children's progress at a bit of a distance and not worry so much about their woes. The world turned and they began to worry more about mine, and I could be cavalier and brush them off and tell them I was fine. Which really I was, by the way. Took the medications of my cohort of age, went about my business.

And in my spare time what did I do? You will now see that I've not always been faithful to my vows. I went back to writing songs. Just a few words at first, jotted down. No melodies, not much. At odd hours when the spirit moved me and I could tell myself they didn't count and weren't songs at all. But really I knew what they were the beginnings of. Car had insisted we have a piano. I began to tap out melodies, one key at a time. I didn't even know how to play a piano. But you know, like all those clichés, the drips of water, the steps of the tortoise, over time my little efforts, mostly in the evenings, maybe with a bit of Armagnac for calm or affectation's sake, began to add up. Don't worry, I'm not going to ply you with those songs, I'm not going to ask you for your opinion. They maybe or maybe not sounded a little like yours. Or a little like somebody's somewhere, or a little like my own. My life was coming full circle.

You'll remember better than I when it was that it appeared in the press how your business manager had robbed you of your life's savings. I guess robbed is a little strong, but defrauded? I remember reading it in the Hollywood Reporter, sitting at my desk, my feet up, and with that view towards Mount Baldy. You were gone from Mount Baldy by then. I knew that, but the view still reminded me of you. Did she cheat you while you were up there praying?

Then I had the thought that, somehow, at last, it was I who could be of some help to you rather than the other way around. If there was one thing I knew about in my years of practice in Los

124

Angeles, it was shady operators, rogue producers, business managers, all manner of hangers-on. I wasn't sure what could be done. It wasn't clear to me if she'd spent all your money or if there were places from which it could still be recovered or even if the papers had all their facts straight. But I knew if the story was true that I could help, particularly if you were now so strapped you couldn't afford to hire a law firm on your own.

I did a bit of research, paid my ten or twenty dollars to some Silicon Valley geniuses, and uncovered that you were most probably living in the Mid-Wilshire district of the city. There were some other Leonard Cohens, members of our little fraternity, living elsewhere around Los Angeles and California, but none of these were close to your age. So I placed my bet. I decided not to try to reach you through any contact in our business, though this might have been the easier path, because I didn't want to appear pushy, or cause embarrassment, or be the butt of some cocktail party gossip. Also, I liked the everyman approach. One citizen to another. I drove directly to your street.

I remember thinking immediately how modest were the houses on your block. Spanish bungalows, little stucco block squares, lawns that needed fertilizer, a few of the lots with chain-link fences around as if three or four feet of chain-link would keep the marauders off. When I found the house number that corresponded to what I'd written on my slip of paper, I was struck that your house was as modest as any of the others. It was neither a monastic hut nor a Hollywood palace. It was like you'd found a middle way. Was that a Buddhist way, I wondered. You see, I was looking out for you then. I was finding evidence and interpreting it in your favor.

There was no car in the driveway. I parked up the block and walked back. I remember how broken the sidewalk paving was. The city had planted the wrong kind of trees. I walked up to your door. I took note that there was some mail in your mailbox. I rang the bell, once, then again. I couldn't hear it ringing inside and no one came to the door, so then I knocked, softly at first, then harder. Again no one came. I waited. I knocked a last time. Then I could see your mail peeping out of the top of the box. Would it really be a violation of the U.S. postal laws to have a look? I pulled the mail out just far enough so that I could see a mailing label: Leonard Cohen.

I took a business card from my wallet and wrote on the back of it: "Call me. I can help." I placed the card at the top of the mailbox, stuffed into the exposed mail so that it wouldn't fall off. Did you ever receive that card? Another question that needs no answer. I waited for your call, or your email, your something. I followed the news about your situation, but it disappeared from even the trades after a little while, as these things do.

To stir my hopes, every so often, I asked myself if I might have gone to the house of the wrong Leonard Cohen, another Leonard Cohen of just your age unknown to the Silicon Valley geniuses. But in your mail there'd been a Hollywood Reporter. No, I had the right one, it was you. And your solution, anyway, when I heard about it a couple of years later, was better than any I could have helped with.

Going back on the road, making millions, being adored. An old guy who could still bring it.

Yours,

Leonard

32

The day he read in the paper that Leonard Cohen had died, Leonard Cohen began to plan his trip. There was no one in the world to whom he could explain this. He might have been able to to Leonard Cohen, he thought. It would have been hard but he might have tried. But Leonard Cohen had died of a fall at night or leukemia or both. The papers didn't seem to be sure. Leonard had retired the year before. He had plenty of time, time even to mourn but he didn't. He had more simply the feeling that life was shutting down, the lights going out. He regretted the undone things in his life. Never to meet that other Leonard Cohen, never to talk to him, never to share the one bad joke which anyway would have puzzled the other. Their names, the difference too, the N and the S, the Norman and Stuart. Who chooses such names? Leonard wondered about the other Leonard Cohen's family. Surely they were mourning. He decided it would be better to return to S. in summer, in August, the month he had been there the once before. Leonard would be seventy-one years old in August. Old enough.

But back to the names. Leonard felt a moment's rush of emotion, almost a choking up, to think of his own mother naming him, or his mother and father both, deciding, satisfied, rather proud. Or Leonard Norman Cohen's parents, wherever they were, she says what about this, he says what about that, arguments and compromises and fresh ideas, somehow it all gets settled, why not Leonard, why not Norman, honoring this one, honoring that one, a blissful moment whether they knew it or not. Or it should have been blissful anyway, to name a child, to think of the future, and Leonard choked up more. The things people omit to notice in their short lives. He and Car the same. Leonard had the thought that since he would be flying east anyway, he should stop off and see the boys. Waste not, want not, and Leonard hated to fly. Then by the time he got around to buying tickets, he had had a further thought. Ah, the internet, what a tool for causing trouble. No, scratch that, why play the cynic when you're getting too old for the part? Leonard located Daphne's brother. He was living in London. He owned a small gallery in London.

He packed as if he were leaving for awhile. He paid the bills and instructed the guy who cut the grass and filled the prescriptions for his blood pressure and cholesterol and talked to a realtor about possibly putting the place up for sale. That would be in the spring, best in the spring. He flew to New York and his dinner with Dave and Mark was perfunctory and bright. An Italian place with a beautiful big veal chop in the Village. Dave was rich, Mark was poor, Dave was on his third start-up, Mark was between gigs, Dave was miserable, Mark seemed happy enough, neither had managed to start a family so there were no grandchildren to coddle or miss. The boys knew where Leonard was going but he didn't tell them why. How beautiful they were. He thought that too. Almost an afterthought, when he was in the cab to the airport.

By the time he got to London, the jet lag was getting to him. It gets worse as you age, everybody says it. He had not contacted Jonathan Sarfatty in advance, being still a believer in just showing up, the element of surprise and all that, plus if you just show up they can't tell you not to come before you're even there. A lawyer's trick perhaps, something he'd picked up along the way. Or a process server's, ugh. Leonard stayed in a very decent hotel, not the best, but very decent. That, too, was his way. In memory, maybe, of the old joke Henny Youngman told, old Jewish guy gets hit by a car, he's lying there, people are helping, ambulance is coming, cop comes by with a pillow for his head, asks "are you comfortable," guy says, "I make a nice living, thank you." And, when he thought of it, wasn't the hotel where he stayed a little like Leonard Cohen's modest house in Mid-Wilshire? Another thing, perhaps, they shared, another something to remember him by. Leonard slept for nine hours, had dinner, then slept till morning. Dreamlessly, it seemed. When he awoke and thought of going to find Jonathan Sarfatty, he felt a little afraid.

Sarfatty was out on an errand when Leonard arrived. It was a narrow gallery across the river in a neighborhood Leonard didn't know, not that he knew the neighborhoods of London, but he knew a handful, the main attractions, from business trips, from a couple of trips with Car. Leonard waited and puzzled himself, amused, by the installations on display. These things, they always looked like something fucking something else. A Rorschach test, maybe, and he would fail every time. The slender girl at the desk ignored him. He waited in a chair and folded his legs. In a half hour a slender man grayed at the temples in a narrow suit of the times returned. Leonard tried to place him with Daphne but it was hard. Cheekbones, sunken cheeks, still a sweep of hair. London had taken all the island out of him. Leonard got out of his chair. It was a warm day and he had his jacket on his arm. Are you Mister Sarfatty, he said.

Sure, he said, and can I help you?

Then he looked to the woman at the desk for help as to who this was, and she shrugged mostly with her eyes so that with luck Leonard wouldn't see.

Then this was all that they said to each other:

You don't know me but I knew your sister. Actually we met once.

You are?

Leonard Cohen. Not *the* Leonard Cohen, of course.

Of course.

It's just been a long confusion in my life.

I can imagine, but so how did you know my sister?

On S. The summer she died.

Sixty-eight.

I was with her. Not when she died. Before.

Before?

Then I came back and she was gone.

Do I remember you?

You were little. In your father's shop.

Actually, yes, I think I do.

Do you?

Well I'm not sure.

It was after the funeral. When your father came back with you.

There was somebody.

There must have been many.

There were. People coming in.

But Americans?

Even Americans, a few.

Did your father hate me? Did he say?

About you?

About anybody? That he hated them.

Why should he have?

I had been her lover. Not for long. But I left, and I came back.

You said.

I'm repeating myself.

He never said anything about you.

Would you remember?

I just don't know.

He's gone now, I assume.

Twenty years.

And the shop?

Gone.

Do you ever go back?

There's no one there for me now.

To S.?

Not to S. There's a resort on Crete.

I see.

So sometimes.

Crete must be pretty.

How can I help you?

I think I just wanted to see you. Sorry, it's a little presumptuous.

I wouldn't say.

Know what you looked like. Know you were alive. Tell you that I was very fond of your sister.

So you were.

I'm sorry.

For what?

I think you know.

But I don't.

But someday maybe you will.

Is that all?

I suppose it is.

I have a meeting. If you would excuse me.

I know it was a long time ago. I know I barged in.

It's not that. But I have a meeting.

Of course.

You know, losing my sister was the worst thing that had ever happened to me.

I can believe that.

And my parents, after all the grief of the war.

She told me about their war.

Or who knows? Maybe they were prepared for anything, after the war, you know?

There might have been more but then there wasn't. Leonard couldn't think what next to say and with a grimace Sarfatty moved past him and down the narrow aisle of the gallery and disappeared while the woman at the desk kept her eyes down.

33

Dear Leonard,

People talk about "sorting things out." But what about sorting out the un-sort-outable?

We go on, we get on the boat. We write letters in the dark with no return address.

Yours,

Leonard

34

The island ferries hadn't changed as much as they might have in fifty years. A little whiter, a little cleaner, but they still bounced along the waves as though they didn't quite belong. There was a fast boat now to S., a hydrofoil, but Leonard would have nothing to do with it. The old-style boat, the deck, the kids a few of whom still looked like hippies, the only way to go in Leonard's heart. He parked his roller bags down below with the backpacks and the rest. It was a pleasant day with a light breeze. The Aegean could also be forgiving. He slept on a bench for awhile and went to the rail at every island stop and stole as many looks as he could at these children all around him who used to be himself. Nobody was playing a guitar, though. The guitars only came out at night. Or so he hoped. He hoped they came out at night. He hoped they weren't passé.

When they came around the western head of S. and into the bay of the town, Leonard was again afraid. He couldn't see the site of the temple atop the cliff, it being high to the east and south so that you'd have to sail past S., towards the next island, to see it, but he knew it was there, awaiting him. In the town there was now a proper port, a broad concrete dock. Quaint *caiques* no longer shuttled travelers in or out. And the ferry was on time, and there was no one for Leonard to joke with about the ferries never being on time. The town had spread up the surrounding hills and looked vast. It wasn't yet dark. A couple of Dutch girls took pity on Leonard when he went to fish out his roller bags from the mountains of luggage by the ferry doors. They found them for him and despite his protests that he was perfectly capable they rolled them off the boat for him as soon as the doors clanked open. On the dock he took his bags back and thanked them and they said good-bye and went off.

35

Dear Leonard,

How the town of S. had changed. I don't know if you ever returned to Hydra, in recent years I mean, but if so I imagine you saw some of the same. ATMs dispensing euros, all-night clubs, all-day bars. My old pension was now a boutique. There were throngs of shoppers. I know there was supposed to be a financial crisis but that August it seemed swept away. Maybe it was only people forgetting about it for a little while, cashing in while they could. A shortage of fish because the sea was mostly fished out, a shortage of lamb because lamb couldn't compete in price with EU chicken and pork, the taverna owners complaining about it all. And the Greek girls wore short skirts and were as made-up as everybody else. Daphne, I thought, would have been appalled. What would Daphne even have looked like if then was now?

The old bookstore was now an all-night pharmacy with a green neon sign and it had absorbed the storefront next door. The hotel where I stayed didn't say on its website that it overlooked the nightclub district and my room was rattled till six in the morning by hip-hop in every language. Would it be indiscreet for me to admit that I've never quite been a fan? I tried, I did try, when I was at Babbington and we had those clients and I could see what was coming down the road. But mostly I kept quiet. Now it kept me up all night, and I was asking myself why I hadn't gone directly to the cliff. Small bands of kids drifted home in the early morning. I peeked through my curtain. Loose and exhausted, weaving along, they looked like they'd had a good time, a once-in-a-short-life time. But there wasn't a rooster crowing anywhere. No more roosters. I wished the kids could hear a rooster crow.

Finally I got a little sleep. Woke up at ten, breakfast, double coffee. Facing the day, a phrase I never particularly liked. It kind of makes the day sound like an enemy, don't you think? Though in this case maybe it was. I'd procrastinated the night before, now I was procrastinating again. It felt like I'd made a date with my own insanity. Hi, how are you, long time no see. Instead of going up the path after breakfast, I went back to the little museum that held whatever the expeditions from New York and Berlin had found and left behind from the Temple of Apollo Metameleia. It was one place in the town that looked entirely the same. Possibly a coat of whitewash, nothing more. Though the glass display cases looked even more antiquated, as though fifty years had only caused dust to collect and etch the glass. The drawing of the god with his wreath and his lyre still had that lofty look, still seemed to say fuck-you-can't-you-tell-I'm-a-god. I felt oddly at home, as though at last I'd found a place I remembered. It smelled dank, as it used to.

Now there was nothing left but to do it. I felt fortified by the god. Surely he wouldn't let me go insane. Nor those eminent archeologists from New York and Berlin with their pith helmets and probable affairs with the interns. History had stability. History was in old glass display cases. It didn't suddenly jump out at you like a ghost, it played by rules and all you had to do was stick to them. And so I did, or thought I did, as I left the museum and walked through the new town that crawled its way up the hills until I found the cutoff to Panagia and then the path.

Here, too, there were houses now, houses way off the road, houses climbing up, houses with a view, vacation rentals or *summer places or houses with a couple of olive trees for somebody to retire to. I didn't know, could only guess. But it was not our place anymore, Daphne's and mine, if it had ever been. The only miracle was that I was halfway surprised. And insulted as well. How dare they! Didn't they know? There's a temple to Apollo up there and Daphne and I are its keepers. We say who goes in or out. We keep it to ourselves. Past tense, past tense. As I climbed, I forgot the past tense.*

I had a walking stick for the rutted path. I had a bottle of water, too, and I stopped a couple of times and caught my breath and looked around, because I was seventy-one years old. The Aegean was so bright I could barely look at it. It looked white, it looked silver. And those white houses, once I was above them, were like dots, speckling the world below with light.

As I came towards the top, I could see ahead of me, in place of the old wire fence and gate, a low spread of barbed wire, like an invasive plant, but at intervals cut through. There was a plaque, too, as I came closer, in Greek and English, ruined like the barbed wire, so badly in need of paint that I could hardly read it. 'APOLLO TEMPLE', 6th Century B.C. Not Admission After Dark. *A failed attraction, a tourist site no one wanted to come to. A few bits of column had been put on top of other bits of column, if they were bits of column at all. And there was trash around, not much but some, plastic water bottles, a couple of beer cans, cardboard. The "Not" on the sign instead of "No," as if teach me no English and I'll tell you no lies.*

I found the closest place where the barbed wire was cut and walked through, pushing the wire away with my stick. And there right in front of me was the slab. It looked like something you might sacrifice something on. I wondered if I had ever noticed before how unnatural its flatness was, as though when the stone was first discovered people could have found in it the stopping place of a god. What had I been thinking? What had I ever noticed? The world then had been like a given, and now it felt taken away. Or is that too trite, too easy? I longed for a do-over. Leave it at that.

And then I saw the tree, not a figment at all, not a surprise, not improbable, but grown to maturity. It clung to the cliff face. It had grown out into the wind, a beautiful, bushy laurel tree, defiant and silent over the water.

Yours,

Leonard

36

Dear Leonard,

Do you know what a laurel tree looks like? Fifty years ago I didn't. But it's the bushiest tree imaginable, if you don't prune it, if you just let it go. Nobody had pruned the tree that was Daphne. She was twenty feet tall and her branches were as thick as her hair. Welcoming, embracing, zaftig, Daphne had been zaftig, and this tree was zaftig, too. The scent of her leaves, defiant, indefinable, pregnant. Such a common leaf, but what a beauty, so dark and glossy, like it had almost seduced the sun. Nor did the tree look old, the way I felt old. It looked in the prime of life, it still had a ways to go. Do you remember ever taking the bay leaves out of a sauce because people said you would choke on them if you left them in? That was Daphne you didn't eat, Daphne who left her flavor and scent and was saved.

I sat down on the ground by the cliff's edge. It was hard ground and my ass was flat and for once I barely shifted as I sat. The meltemi had died and the sea was still as bright as bottled lightning. In the heat of the afternoon the shapes of neighboring islands seemed to quiver on the horizon. I waited for the tree to say "Len-ny," I waited for the miracle, as if miracles happened twice. But all I heard were the lightest of breezes in her branches.

Daphne, I asked, Daphne, are you there? I said it out loud but I could have said it in my head and would it have made any difference? Faith or insanity, take your pick, one or the other but you can't have both.

My god, I felt so stupid then, hearing my voice. It would have been one thing if she had answered back, but she didn't. The tree could have been mocking me, having the last laugh, tittering in its leaves, or the tree could have been nothing but a tree. And yet I continued. I was going to have my say. It had been so long and I felt in the presence of a friend. Can a tree be your friend? I suppose it can, especially if you have no other friend. Are you my friend, Leonard? Is that why I'm telling you this tale, my friend at long last, when it's too late to say the least?

I've missed you, Daphne, I said.

And how's that for trite, I said.

I've lived a life without you, I said, and then I told her a little about my life, things I needn't repeat here.

I told her about you, too, Leonard, about how I went to the monastery and went to your house and no one came to the door.

He died, you know, I said.

I'm not sure if you keep up on the world or not, I said. I'm not sure how all this works. So forgive me if you already know, or stop me, feel free to interrupt, I said.

But she didn't stop me, she didn't interrupt.

After he died was when I decided to come see you, I said.

I had no idea what this would be like, I said.

I stopped in London and saw your brother, he's living there now, I said, and I told her all I knew about her little brother, the little I knew, really, but how beautiful he was. I wanted her to know that he was still beautiful. Though it's true that I was half thinking of my own sons then.

I told her about Winston being in the CIA. You were right about that one, I said.

The bookshop's gone now, I said.

Nobody to take it, I guess, I said.

And I told her about the changes to the island, in case she hadn't heard, in case she couldn't see.

There's a new ferry boat now, I said.

And there's a dock so they can steam right in, I said.

In America bay leaves are in fashion, I said.

Americans are still fairly arrogant, I said, and added that I didn't think she'd be surprised by that.

If I had taken you to Philadelphia, if you'd come with me to Philadelphia, I don't know what would have happened, I said, but if we had gotten past that part of it we could be a funny old couple by now, starting to get slightly forgetful, fifty years married. Maybe, maybe not, I said.

And as for Apollo, I said. My personal opinion about Apollo. I've had time, you see, decades really, to form an opinion about that guy from the slab. From his loss of Daphne came the birth of love out of lust. And I didn't just read that somewhere, I really believe it, I said. It was one of the things I believed, I said, and I didn't believe too many.

The weather, the time of day, I talked about those too. I was trying to keep something going. Just keep talking and it won't end.

And I asked her things. Not that I expected a response. By then I expected no answers to anything. But I asked her about being a tree, about treeness, and if she was actually a tree or was she a girl trapped in a tree, then I apologized for trying to think such things through, for thinking that by thinking alone such things can be known.

I came back when I said I would, I said.

I came back and you were gone, I said.

Could I ask you one thing more, I said. I've thought about it so long that there were even times when I forgot about it.

But did you jump off the cliff or did you slip? I asked.

I always thought you slipped, I said.

I wanted to think that, I said.

I heard nothing at all come from the tree and by then I was very tired, from the heat of the day, from not having slept the night before, from still a touch of the jet lag, from having spoken too long about too many things. Or was it only that my long wait was over?

I stretched out on the hard ground.

You're looking very well, I said.

I wish I could say the same for myself, I said.

I curled myself by her side, reached out with one hand and placed it on her trunk, which was cool and smooth, and fell into the peace of a long siesta.

Yours,

Leonard

37

Dear Leonard,

I was awakened by our name. No, more truthfully, I was awakened by her voice. Len-ny, Len-ny, it called, as if it were calling me home. The lilt of it, the friendly insistence. How much music she found in our name. No one had ever called me so sweetly. Len-ny, are you going to sleep the whole night?

Though it was also true that her voice sounded older, deeper, as if it had been exposed both to the weather and the years.

It was dark now. I looked around, as though to see if she could have thrown her voice, as if to seek out the magic in the miracle. My hand still touched her bark. I looked up into her branches. I smiled a doubter's smile. Did you say something, I said.

Are you going to sleep the whole night? I heard again. Look what time is it.

You're here! You're alive! I shouted.

Letting go of her trunk, I looked deeper into the branches, as if I might see her face in them, construct it somehow, or it would simply be there. But I could see only branches, black against a black sky.

Then I heard: Where is your guitar?

What?

Your guitar!

So you're still here. I thought you might have gone.

Don't be silly. Where can I go? Len-ny, I want you to play me a song.

I don't have a guitar anymore, I said.

Go get one of course, she said.

How can I get one? The stores are closed by now, I said.

Of course they're not closed, she said.

Are we going to have an argument after fifty years, I said.

Who starts arguments, she said.

The path's too dark, I said.

Go by the moonlight, she said.

There is no moonlight, I said.

But I had hardly got out the words when whatever cloud had covered it slipped away from the moon.

You never believe me, she said.

I'll be back, I said, though really I hated to leave, afraid that by the time I returned, the spell would be broken.

I negotiated the barbed wire and started down the path of ruts and stones. Would you agree with something, Leonard? Once something impossible happens, anything else impossible can happen. I took my walking stick with me. I was like a goat in the moonlight. My only thought was Daphne's voice and getting back to it before it was gone.

It was past ten in S. and the cafés were shutting and the clubs were opening. As for the shops, they all seemed closed, and I wondered how many places on S. would anyway have a guitar. I looked around for a kid I might borrow or beg one from. I asked about shops. Everyone said everything was shut and I wandered around forlorn or actually a little put out by the wild goose chase, or thinking even if it was Daphne's way to get rid of me. But on the block of the old bookshop, up from the pharmacy, there was a junk dealer's stall, lit by a single bulb. I say junk dealer, but really I couldn't tell what it was. Possibly a pawn shop. Possibly the guy recycled. But I saw the light and the narrow opening to the stall and a couple of barrels outside and I went in. On a shelf, along with a trumpet and a forty-five record player and a couple of cheap speakers, was an old guitar. The proprietor looked like he'd come out of the Crete mountains. I didn't even know they still had such guys. Rough guys, swords and vendetta guys. Or maybe it was all for show, give the tourists a run for their money. I pointed to the guitar and paid him whatever he asked. It was a terrible guitar but I tuned it a little and it halfway tuned up and anyway it was all there was.

I climbed back to the Panagia road and then up the path. Now the moon was coming in and out but my eyes were better and I picked my way along, with my walking stick and my guitar slung over. Old guy can still do it, like you going back on tour. I praised myself a little that way. And I prayed that she, the voice, the miracle, whatever it was, would still be there.

Daphne, I called, as I came through the break in the barbed wire.

Len-ny, come look, she called back.

Come look at what, I asked, then I came closer to the edge of the cliff and the tree and from there I could see the ferry from S. making its way across the sea. Its strings of white pearls glistened. It seemed very far away.

I see it every night, Daphne said.

I'm glad, I said.

Of course you found the shop, she said.

I did, of course, I said.

Was it so hard, poor Len-ny, she said.

It's a terrible guitar, I said.

What would you like to play me, she said.

Whatever you like, I said.

Leonard Cohen, she said.

The sea was peaceful that night. So far, far below my feet, it seemed to beckon, as I imagined it must have beckoned Daphne once. I took a step back from the cliff.

Then I tuned the guitar a little more, got it as close as it would come, then I played your songs, and sang them too, in my scratchy old Jew's voice. I felt like a shepherd without a flock. Or a boy with his love. I sang "Suzanne." I sang "Dance Me to the End of Time." I sang "Everybody Knows." I sang "Bird on the Wire," "You Want It Darker," "I'm Your Man." I sang "So Long, Marianne." Do I owe you a royalty? I wonder how that goes. I wonder if you play for a girl in a tree whether the regular rates apply? A ghost in a tree. Ask Cohen, ask Lenny Cohen over at Babbington, he ought to know.

Though what happened to him? He's gone. Haven't seen him in awhile. All the Leonard Cohens are gone.

Daphne said little while I sang but I believed that she was listening. What a wonderful thing faith is and the most amazing thing is you can't explain it to anyone. It doesn't compute. Daphne never computed. I should have been saving up for law school that summer. I should have been going to Vietnam.

More? I finally said.

Enough, she said.

Then I didn't know what more to say or to do.

It was Daphne who broke the silence that could have been our code for "enough." I asked for Leonard Cohen, she said.

But I played you Leonard Cohen, I said.

But I want <u>my</u> Leonard Cohen, she said.

I don't have anything to sing you. Nothing that's good enough, nothing that I want you to hear, I said.

Do you remember when you told me your big wish to write one song as good as his? she said.

Of course I do, I said.

Then first you need a wreath, she said.

Excuse me? I said.

Please, now, you must make a wreath, she said.

Why would I do that, I said.

Because I ask you to, she said. I beg you, I plead you, can you see me on my knees?

I don't deserve a wreath, I said.

Nonsense, she said.

Wreaths are for victors, I said.

My leaves are for who I give them to, she said.

Will you give them to me then, I said.

Pick my leaves and wreathe them how I tell you to, she said.

So I did. I put down the guitar and picked a handful of her leaves. They were like dark green gold, little flakes of dark green gold, in my hands.

But how do I string them together? I asked.

Use a string of your guitar, she said. You won't be needing it now, she said.

So again I did what she said, whether it sounded silly or it didn't, a chewing-gum kind of fix, but I strung the guitar string through the leaves, and bit off the excess string to make a proper length, and tied the two ends that were left together. It was a pretty terrible wreath, as terrible as the guitar, but it was mine. That's what Daphne said, anyway, when I was done.

Why did you say I won't need the guitar? I asked.

Put the wreath on your head, she said.

Is this a costume ball, I said.

Now you look like a god, she said, when it was crooked on my head.

Oh please, I said.

You think I make fun of you, she said.

Maybe, is it true, I said.

Now you can write your beautiful song, she said. As good a song as one of his, she said.

How am I going to do that, I said.

Come closer to me, she said.

I've never managed to write one till now, I said.

Come closer, she said.

Is it true, I said.

Is what true, she said.

What you just said, I said.

That you could write one as good as his?

As good as any one of his, even the least of his.

Of course.

But how?

Come closer, I say.

So I did. And when I reached out to put my arms around her trunk to embrace her, it seemed like her branches were embracing me.

I kissed her smooth bark.

Then she began with a little introduction. This will be your song, she said. Len-ny's song, only Len-ny's song, and it will be as good and as beautiful as anyone's song. My Leonard Cohen, my sweet Leonard Cohen. And as soon as she began to sing, in a voice that I knew too well and yet, suddenly, not at all, a case if there ever was of those who have ears to hear, I knew that it had to be true, that it would be my song alone, just like she said. I would hear it and no one else ever would. And whether it was as good a song as one of yours, or as beautiful, I would never have to say, not in eons, not in all eternity, because she had said it was, and so it was.

And that's all I remember, except that as I held the tree with all I had and listened, I felt like I had fallen off a cliff without even knowing if I had slipped or jumped.

Yours,

Leonard

38

Dear Leonard,

Let me throw out an alternative version of the case. A bubbe meise, if you will. You think it was me who wrote all these letters to you, but what if it wasn't?

I'm assuming, of course, that you've thought about this at all, which I understand by some could be thought to be improbable.

But let's just say. What if fifty years ago I returned to S. as I said I would and found that Daphne was simply gone? What if no fisherman had found a body because there wasn't a body to be found? What if she had instead got on the boat to Piraeus, telling no one, because she had her life to live? On the boat she sat on the deck a little apart from the hippies and foreigners and watched them. She was young, in her dark way she was beautiful, little conversations started and soon somebody had a guitar or a banjo or zither and she was singing along. She had one of those deep Greek voices and there were others who listened. From Athens she notified her family, because she wasn't the type to be cruel. She got a job, this or that, then someone heard her voice again and she was hired in the Plaka to sing for the tourists, the songs of others but also her own. She took entrance exams to the university. She was admitted and was kind of a star. She studied, say, anthropology and went to Paris. While getting still one more degree she met a French guy and later they had children and raised them with all the proper left-wing views and then they divorced. She taught somewhere. In the evenings she went back to writing songs, a few anyway, and on a lark she sang Tuesday nights in a place a friend owned. Her voice was still pretty good, it was low and a little mocking, the songs were political or about love. She was alone. There were a few more lovers along the way. She got a fellowship to America and landed at UCLA. This was 2016 and she read that you had died. It reminded her if she needed reminding. She found out my house in the Palisades. She drove there and parked on the street and rang the bell and when no one came to the door she peeked through the windows to be sure. Then she put the song she'd written the night before about a summer love on top of my mailbox, tucked in a little among the circulars from the grocery stores, but it blew away. It was as good a song as one of yours, she thought at first, but then she didn't care, if it was or if it wasn't. It was only an ironic thought anyway. Later she returned to S. She hadn't been there in all the years. She noted the changes, she mourned the bookshop that was gone. One evening she went up the path to the ruined temple. She stood at the edge of the cliff and watched the lights of the ferry, then lay down on the slab and began to write, all these letters, that you've read or not read, as if it were all her great reversal of fortune. She didn't return to Paris until she was done.

None of this was so, this bubbe meise, this twist of an old tale. But it would have been, I think, more just if it was. I wonder if I have even the right to talk about justice when it comes to Daphne. But give credit where credit is due, they say, and justice is in short supply, in as short supply as love. She might even have planted a young laurel tree at the edge of the cliff.

Yours,

Leonard

39

The way his body was found, a few people wondered what had gone on. It was wound so tightly around the tree. It seemed to be an embrace, but why would he embrace a tree? And what was going on with the laurel wreath that was found, crooked on his head? Boys discovered the body, their first days off from school, off for a hike, on a warm June day when the asphodels were in bloom. Neither of them had seen a dead person before. They went to their parents, then with their parents to the police office. No autopsy was performed, there being no facility on the island to perform one, though a local doctor examined the corpse and found no evidence of violence. The assumption, given the deceased's age and medications, was heart failure. The doctor pronounced that that was the case. The commanding police officer speculated that in the United States there were such things as "tree huggers," so perhaps the deceased had been one of those, and perhaps that would explain the wreath as well, though the police officer couldn't say how. There was also some confusion as to the name on the passport. At first there were those, such as the doctor's nurse, who became excited over the possibility that a celebrity had died in their midst. It took a little while to determine that the celebrity had died two years before and was anyway Canadian.

As much mystery as clarification was then provided when Dmitris of the Kafeneion Olympus, by the waterfront, reported that one Leonard Cohen, not *the* Leonard Cohen but another one, had been coming into his café all through the fall and winter months, sipping one Fanta after another and much of the time scribbling on yellow pads. No such yellow pads were subsequently found. A resident of the Panagia road said he had seen the same foreigner many nights at dusk mounting the dirt path to the temple and sometimes had observed him as well in the morning coming down. The pension owner who turned over Leonard's things admitted that the man kept puzzling hours but was otherwise no trouble and paid on time. This was as much investigation as was done, as the deteriorating condition of the remains required prompt action. The passport was processed, the United States embassy in Athens notified, two sons in New York found, and arrangements made for the body to be shipped by helicopter to Athens, then onward. In Los Angeles, customs agents seized the wreath that had been included among Leonard's personal effects because it was alien plant life that was not permitted entry according to Department of Agriculture regulations.

40

Leonard's sons grieved for a father they remembered as decent, though of course grief is a complicated thing. They had everyday, unspectacular memories, ballgames, vacations, school events. A guy who showed up. Leonard was cremated. Mark had taken up a bit of Judaism and said it was against Jewish law, but a wish for cremation was in Leonard's will and he and Car had always talked about cremation and so that's what was done. Then there was a memorial service in a mountain setting in Malibu that was available for such things. It was a small affair. The boys, Car, colleagues from Babbington, neighborhood friends, a few relations Leonard scarcely knew who lived near San Diego, a couple of clients. Of his old friends from Penn, Harv Pressman showed up. Harv had had a bumpy ride, which was how he described it if anyone ever asked, three failed marriages and now Parkinson's coming on. But he was cheerful enough, wearing a hat against the Malibu sun.

A rabbi pronounced a few platitudes and talked about Leonard's love of music. He'd been given notes as to what to say about a man he had never met. A string quartet played Brahms. Various law partners recalled Leonard's good nature and his victory in the Goldstein Bakery case as well as his contributions to palimony law. A junior associate told how Leonard had nurtured him. Dave spoke about his father's love of music, and his apparent love of Greece, having spent his last months there. Mark struck the only slightly discord-ant note when he said, after noting his father's kindnesses, that perhaps he had given too much to others and had never fulfilled his own heart's desire. Mark was still the hippie at heart. Then the string quartet played again and the rabbi said the prayer for the dead and a student from the music school downtown sang her version of Leonard Cohen's "Hallelujah," which was understood by pretty much all in attendance to be appropriate enough for "our" Leonard Cohen.

Afterwards, driving back to the house in the Palisades where they were staying, Dave asked Mark why he had said that their father had not fulfilled his heart's desire. It just seemed to him that's how it was, Mark said. Dave asked what he was talking about specifically. Mark said he wasn't sure. Dave said if there was something their father wanted to do, he would have done it, and going back to Greece was evidence of it. Mark said it could also be evidence of exactly the opposite, if he went back too late. What's too late, Dave said. Mark said he didn't know.

THE END